a melody of contrasts
A BWWM ROMANCE

SAVANNAH KOLE

ARDENT ARTIST BOOKS

A Melody of Contrasts
Copyright © 2024 by Savannah Kole
All rights reserved.

Book Cover and formatting provided by Trisha Fuentes
https://bit.ly/m/trishafuentes

No part of this book may be reproduced in any form or by any electronic or mechanical means, including information storage and retrieval systems, without written permission from the author, except for the use of brief quotations in a book review.

ISBN: 979-8-8691-6054-6 (Paperback)

**Published by
Ardent Artist Books**
www.ardentartistbooks.com

other books published by ardent artist books

✦Modern Romance✦
Offsides
Cougar at Play
Love Child - Part 1
Love Child - Part 2
Mystique
Kisser
Taunt Me
Sing Me a Song
Jealousy Never Looked So Good
Almost Yours
A Test for True Love
A Melody of Contrasts
Hidden Depths
Crowded
Meet Me on Social Media
The Butterfly
Pop Fly Kiss
Curves
Forbidden Love

She Was Going Home
A Sacrifice Play
Faded Dreams
Never Say Forever

✦Historical Romance✦

The Anzan Heir
Magnet & Steele
The Relentless Rogue
One Starry Night
In The Moonlight With You
Captivating the Captain
The Merry Widow
Unrequited Love
The Summer Romance of the Duke
Love Without Warning
Love in Winter

✦✦SERIES✦✦
DOLLAR•PRINCESS

The Penny Bride - Book 1
The Misguided Bride - Book 2
The Marquess Made For Me - Book 3

HOLLINGER

Dare To Love - Book 1
A Matchless Match - Book 2
Arrogance & Conceit - Book 3
Impropriety - Book 4

SERVICE•DAUGHTER

The Steward's Daughter - Book 1
The Cook's Daughter - Book 2
The Curator's Daughter - Book 3

THUNDERBOLT
The Surprise Heir - Book 1
A Dance of Deception - Book 2
Win the Heart of a Duchess - Book 3

OBSESSION
Unsuitable Obsession - Part One
Broken Obsession - Part Two

ESCAPE
Swept Away - Book 1
Fire & Rescue - Book 2
The Domain King - Book 3

LATIN•LADIES
The Family Fix - Book 1
A Taste of Fire - Book 2
Songs of the Heart - Book 3

THE•PROTECTOR
The Dark Side of Him - Book 1
Guarded by Shadows - Book 2
Tangled Loyalties - Book 3

CROSSOVER•CHARACTERS
The Bargain Bride - Book 1
Evenly Matched - Book 2
Second in Command - Book 3

AGE•GAP•ROMANCE
His Encore, Her Ecstasy - Book 1
Whispers of Yesterday - Book 2
Against the Wind - Book 3

contents

Chapter 1	1
Chapter 2	9
Chapter 3	19
Chapter 4	29
Chapter 5	39
Chapter 6	49
Chapter 7	57
Chapter 8	67
Chapter 9	75
Chapter 10	87
Chapter 11	95
Chapter 12	105
Chapter 13	115
Chapter 14	123
Chapter 15	133
Chapter 16	141
Acknowledgments	147
Subscribe to our Newsletter	149
Hidden Depths	151
The Family Fix	153
A Test for True Love	155
Also by Savannah	157
About Savannah	159

one

LOS ANGELES, CALIFORNIA

The spotlight's harsh glare illuminated Prissy's slender form, her cello cradled between her thighs like a cherished lover. The polished wood gleamed, the curved body an invitation to pluck its strings and unleash a carnal symphony.

A low murmur thrummed through Mo's Jazz Club, patrons clinking glasses in hushed anticipation. Cigarette smoke coiled lazily in the low lighting, mingling with the heady scent of whiskey and desire.

Prissy took a deep breath, feeling the heaviness of her instrument bring her back down to earth. The chaos outside the stage became background noise as she immersed herself in the intimate moment. Giving a slight nod to the saxophonist, she tightened her bow against the strings.

The jazz quartet was a harmonious blend of elegant instruments - her cello, the resonant piano, the sultry saxophonist and the rhythmic drums. Night after night, this was her life's work, delightfully sharing her musical prowess with the enthusiastic crowds who eagerly paid twenty dollars at the door for the pleasure of listening. The passion in their performance was palpable as each note danced through the air, filling every corner of the room with enchanting melodies.

Prissy's intense gaze challenged the captivated audience as she skillfully played the strings, coaxing out passionate melodies. Her fingers moved with urgency, commanding the strings to submit to her every command.

As the final, quivering note evaporated into silence, Prissy held the crowd in the palm of her hand, bound by desires too exquisite to vocalize. A single bead of sweat traced the graceful line of her throat as she drank in their ravenous hunger.

The crowd erupted in thunderous applause, shattering the delicious tension. Prissy allowed the faintest of smiles to grace her full lips as she surrendered to the roar of adulation.

She wanted their adoration, but a feeling of emptiness gnawed at her. Despite the applause and praise, she couldn't shake the ache inside when the music ended. It was her burden to carry - a master at portraying emotions, but lacking them in her own life.

Prissy's gaze drifted over the enraptured masses, seeking solace in the faceless crowd. Her smoldering eyes alighted upon a striking figure, conspicuous amidst the drab scenery. An imposing man regarded her with unabashed want, his chiseled features etched in shadow.

A shiver ran down her spine as they locked eyes. In that tense moment, she could see herself in his hungry gaze - a desire for the pleasure she had just sold without shame. An unspoken dare sparked between them, igniting forbidden desires.

Prissy snapped out of her daze, her heart beating with desire. She scolded herself for even considering getting involved. It would only end in disaster. But the intense urge coursed through her veins, longing for something more than just music.

The soulful strains of the piano drifted through the smoky haze, beckoning Prissy back into the moment. With a subtle nod, she cued the drummer, her bow poised over the strings like a matador's blade. The sultry notes spilled forth, slicing through the cloying air with surgical precision.

The smooth, sultry notes of the jazz quartet drifted through the air, captivating the audience with their enchanting melody. As their set came to an end, the three other musicians gracefully left the stage, leaving Prissy alone in the spotlight for her solo.

The hush that fell over the crowd was palpable as the announcer's voice boomed through the speakers, calling everyone's attention to the next performance. "Ladies and gentlemen," he announced, his voice dripping with excitement and anticipation. "I give you, the talented and mesmerizing, Prissy Alexander."

Prissy flashed a bright smile before closing her eyes and focusing on her instrument. With each note she played, she poured her heart and soul into the music, her fingers dancing along the keys with effortless grace. The hauntingly beautiful sound of *"Caruso"* filled the room, carrying everyone away on a journey of emotions.

Her eyelids fluttered closed as the music enveloped her, shutting out all distractions. The cello became an extension of her being, its woodsy lamentations a mere echo of the anguished melodies unfurling within her. Each sweeping crescendo, each quivering vibrato, bled from the depths of her lonely heart.

Prissy let the music take over, her body moving in sync with the passionate beats. Her skilled fingers guided the bow across the strings, creating each note with precision.

This was her lifelong dream, the one she had diligently pursued since the tender age of ten. To stand alone, center stage, commanding the undivided attention of an audience as a soloist. It was what drove her to practice tirelessly and study endlessly, honing her craft until she was ready to take on the world with her own show. The thought alone filled her with a sense of excitement and determination, propelling her further towards her ultimate goal.

Lost in the music, everything else faded away. It was just her and her instrument, entwined in a passionate embrace. The cello cried out, expressing the forbidden desires she could never speak aloud. Sweat glistened on Prissy's forehead as she reached the climax, her flushed skin showing the intensity of her emotions. With a final exhale, she surrendered to the wave, her body trembling with release.

Chest heaving, she held the last quavering note until it dissipated into the ether, leaving only a charged silence tingling in its wake. As the spell broke, Prissy's eyes fluttered open, dark pools glistening with unspent desire.

The heavy silence that followed Prissy's spellbinding performance was swiftly shattered by thunderous applause. A tide of adulation washed over her as the enraptured audience erupted in a frenzy of appreciation.

Countless faces looked up at her, their emotions on display. Some held their chests and teared up, as if her sad song stirred deep sorrows. Others beamed with happiness, moved by her joyful performance.

At the front row, an old couple held hands, their aged faces filled with nostalgia as Prissy's melodies took them back to precious memories. Behind them sat a young woman biting her lip, clutching onto the soft armrest as if trying to anchor herself against the emotional waves stirred by the cellist's mournful songs.

Despite the crowd's overwhelming applause, Prissy couldn't shake the emptiness inside her. She had sacrificed everything for her music, even relationships that now seemed like distant memories. With the deafening cheers ringing in her ears, she wondered if it was all worth it in the end.

As the applause died down, Prissy took a deep breath and lowered her cello. She ran her fingers over its smooth surface, seeking comfort in its familiarity.

The announcer stepped back on stage and took the

microphone. "Prissy Alexander, everyone," he said, clapping and turning towards her with a smile. "Our piano will return after a brief remission."

Prissy scanned the crowded jazz club and saw happy faces, couples wrapped in each other's arms, and friends laughing and toasting. She felt a twinge of sadness as she longed for that kind of connection. With a heavy heart, she left the stage with her cello in hand. Backstage was quiet compared to the lively atmosphere of the club. As she put away her instrument, she couldn't help but feel familiar feelings of loneliness after a successful performance. All the hard work and sacrifices had brought her to where she was now – at the top of her career. Yet, as she undressed, Prissy couldn't shake off the nagging feeling that something important was still missing, an untouched part of her soul that music could not heal.

The dressing room seemed to close in around her, the air thick with the lingering scent of sweat and greasepaint. Prissy found herself pacing the confined space, her fingers restlessly toying with the pearls at her throat – a nervous habit she could never quite break.

Prissy's expression darkened at the sight of her worn cello case. She had given up so much for her music, but it was a sacrifice she couldn't resist.

With a resigned sigh, she hefted the case onto her shoulder, the familiar weight a comforting anchor in the maelstrom of her turbulent emotions. As she made her way towards the exit, her steps were heavier, weighted down by the knowledge that tonight's performance was just another chapter in an endless cycle of euphoria and disillusionment.

Prissy stepped out of the backstage area and into Mo's Jazz Club. The room was filled with the usual noise - glasses clinking, people laughing and talking loudly. She made her way through the tables, still buzzing from her intense performance. Her hand absentmindedly traced her cello case, a constant companion throughout her unpredictable career. Despite the accolades, she couldn't shake the feeling of emptiness inside, always yearning for something beyond temporary applause.

As she neared the exit, a familiar voice cut through the din, causing her to falter mid-stride. "Leaving so soon, darlin'?" Maurice's syrupy drawl oozed with the same unsubtle undertones that had become his calling card over the years. "Surely you can spare a moment for an old friend."

Prissy's jaw clenched imperceptibly as she pivoted to face the club owner, her expression a carefully curated mask of polite disinterest. Maurice lounged against the bar, his immaculately tailored suit a stark contrast to the roguish glint in his eye as he appraised her with unbridled appreciation.

"You were magnificent tonight, as always," he purred, languidly nursing a tumbler of amber liquid. "Though I must admit, I never truly appreciated the...sensual nature of the cello until you graced my humble establishment with your talents."

A contemptuous retort danced on the tip of Prissy's tongue, but she swallowed it down, painfully aware of the delicate dance required to maintain her tenuous position in Maurice's good graces. Her reputation, her livelihood, hinged on playing by his rules, no matter how demeaning or degrading.

With a tight smile, she inclined her head in a polite nod. "I live to perform, Maurice. You know that." The words felt like ash in her mouth, but she persevered, unwilling to relinquish the slim foothold she had managed to carve out in this unforgiving world.

As their eyes locked, a silent challenge passed between them – Maurice's gaze an unspoken promise of the depravities to which he could stoop, while Prissy's smoldered with a defiant vow to never truly surrender her soul to his whims.

Prissy was at a stalemate, and it made her uneasy. She knew men like Maurice saw her as an object to be used, not as an artist. But giving up her passion for art was out of the question, even if it meant facing a soul-crushing reality.

On stage, with her cello in hand, she was transported to another world where nothing else existed except for the emotional power of the music. It was her only escape, a safe haven where she could immerse herself in each note and express her innermost desires without words.

A wistful smile tugged at the corners of her lips as she reminisced about the thrill of holding the audience in the palm of her hand, their captivated faces a testament to the power of her artistry. In those moments, she was more than just a woman with a cello – she was a conduit for something transcendent, a storyteller weaving tales that resonated in the very depths of the human soul.

Yet, as the final notes faded into silence, reality would inevitably come crashing back. The harsh glare of the spotlight, the leering gazes of men like Maurice, the relentless demands of a career that consumed her every waking hour – it was a brutal reminder that her life was a constant tightrope walk between personal fulfillment and soul-crushing compromise.

She nodded and walked towards the exit, her cello case feeling heavier as she carried the weight of a life balancing compromise and integrity.

Prissy felt the cool night air on her face, a reminder of the delicate balance between success and failure in her life. She was used to living on the edge as an artist, but as she grew older, it became even more precarious.

As Prissy walked down the deserted streets, she felt determined to face whatever challenges lay ahead. With her cello by her side, she was ready to create a fulfilling life using the magic of her music. It wouldn't be easy, but she was driven by the same passion that had defined her artistry thus far.

two

The grand doors swung open, and all eyes turned towards the entrance as Alex Shefton strode into the gallery. His presence commanded attention, a magnetic aura that drew whispers and admiring glances from the well-heeled crowd. With a tailored suit that accentuated his lean frame and impeccable posture, he exuded an air of refined sophistication. Each step echoed with a sense of purpose, as if the marble floor beneath his feet was a stage upon which he performed the role of the distinguished art connoisseur to perfection.

Alex's gaze swept across the room, taking in the exquisite pieces adorning the walls. A faint smirk played upon his lips as he recognized the subtle brushstrokes and color palettes of masters long revered. He made his way towards a small cluster of fellow enthusiasts, exchanging cordial nods and pleasantries with the ease of a seasoned socialite.

"Ah, Percival, delightful to see you here," Alex greeted an older gentleman with a firm handshake. "I trust you've had the opportunity to appreciate the Renoir in the east wing? Exquisite, wouldn't you say?"

Percival's eyes lit up, eagerly engaging in the discourse. "Indeed, my dear fellow. The way he captured the interplay of light and shadow is simply breathtaking. Though, I must confess, the Monet landscapes have quite captured my fancy this evening."

Alex chuckled, a low rumble that hinted at his appreciation for the finer things in life. "Ah, yes, the master of impressionism. One can almost feel the gentle breeze caressing the canvas." His gaze flickered briefly towards a striking portrait, and a fleeting crease formed between his brows, but he swiftly regained his composure.

As the conversation flowed like a delicate dance, Alex effortlessly wove in anecdotes and insights, showcasing his vast knowledge and passion for the art world. Each word was carefully chosen, a delicate balance between erudition and charm, captivating his audience with the artistry of his speech.

As the conversation lulled, Alex excused himself politely, his keen eye drawn to a stern-faced woman standing before a monumental abstract canvas. Her gaze was transfixed, as if she had become a part of the painting itself. Alex recognized her instantly – Elise Moreau, the celebrated French avant-garde artist whose bold strokes and unorthodox techniques had stirred controversy and admiration in equal measure.

Emboldened by his insatiable curiosity, Alex approached her with a respectful nod. "Mademoiselle Moreau, it's an honor to bask in the presence of such a visionary talent," he remarked, his voice rich with genuine appreciation.

Elise turned, regarding him with a penetrating stare that seemed to pierce through his immaculate facade. "Monsieur Shefton," she acknowledged, her tone clipped yet intrigued. "I must admit, I'm surprised to find a connoisseur of your... refined tastes appreciating my work."

A faint smile played upon Alex's lips, undeterred by her directness. "Art transcends boundaries, does it not? True beauty lies in the artist's ability to evoke emotion, to challenge the very essence of perception." He gestured towards the canvas, his eyes alight with intellectual fervor. "Pray, indulge me, Mademoiselle. What inspired this audacious masterpiece?"

Elise's gaze softened ever so slightly, and she launched into a passionate discourse, her words flowing like brushstrokes upon a blank canvas. Alex listened intently, his mind absorbing every nuance, every stroke of her creative process. He posed thoughtful questions, probing the depths of her artistic philosophy, and engaged in a spirited exchange that left them both invigorated.

As their profound tête-à-tête drew to a close, Alex inclined his head in sincere admiration. "Merci, Mademoiselle Moreau. You've opened my eyes to new realms of perception. Truly, art is the bridge that connects our souls."

With a slight upturn of her lips, Elise nodded, a silent acknowledgment of the rare kinship they had shared in that fleeting moment. And as Alex turned away, his steps lighter, his mind brimming with fresh insights, he felt a renewed sense of purpose – to seek out beauty in all its unconventional forms.

Alex strode through the grand exhibition hall, his eyes roving over the assembled guests with a practiced, discerning gaze. Influential art collectors, celebrated critics, and esteemed patrons mingled amidst the breathtaking displays, their murmurs a symphony of cultured appreciation.

With an effortless charm, he engaged in idle banter, exchanging pleasantries and offering insightful observations on the exhibited works. His words flowed with a refined eloquence, each utterance a subtle exhibition of his vast knowledge and keen aesthetic sensibilities.

"Ah, Monsieur Durand," Alex greeted a renowned collector, his voice rich with warmth. "I must commend your exquisite eye. That Renoir you acquired at the Sotheby's auction is an absolute gem. The way the light dances upon the canvas, caressing the curves of the young lady's form – simply breathtaking."

Monsieur Durand's chest puffed with pride. "You have an enviable talent for appreciating the finer details, Monsieur Shefton. It's what sets true connoisseurs apart from mere spectators."

Alex allowed a faint smirk to grace his features. "Indeed. Though I must confess, I've been somewhat...distracted this evening." His gaze flickered towards a particularly striking abstract piece, his brow furrowing ever so slightly.

The colors clashed together in a messy way, defying any sense of structure. Alex's fingers twitched with his need for control and organization.

"You see that one over there?" he murmured, his tone laced with subtle disdain. "The brush strokes are entirely lacking in cohesion. It's as if the artist simply flung paint upon the canvas without rhyme or reason."

Monsieur Durand arched a brow, his expression one of mild amusement. "Ah, but therein lies the beauty, my friend. Art need not conform to rigid structures. It is a expression of raw emotion, a visceral outpouring of the artist's soul."

Alex's jaw clenched, a sign of his control issues. Chaos was not something he could appreciate. Beauty required precision and attention to detail to truly elevate it.

Forcing a tight smile, he gave a curt nod. "Perhaps you're right. I shall endeavor to open my mind to...alternative perspectives." The words tasted bitter on his tongue, a reluctant concession to the unpredictable nature of artistic expression.

Monsieur Durand left and Alex's attention reverted back to the controversial artwork. He clenched his fingers, trying to maintain control. He took a deep breath, fighting the urge to impose order on the chaotic scene.

For a moment, he wavered between giving in to his natural tendencies and embracing the unknown. His internal conflict was evident on his face, a battle of wills within his composed demeanor.

Alex turned away from the unsettling artwork, his jaw still clenched as he sought solace amidst the more conventional pieces adorning the gallery walls. It was then that his gaze fell upon a striking portrait, the bold brushstrokes and vibrant hues seemingly leaping from the canvas to ensnare his senses.

The subject's eyes, rendered in smoldering shades of amber and sienna, exuded a captivating intensity that threatened to pierce the very depths of his soul. Alex found himself drawn inexorably closer, his footsteps measured and purposeful, as if obeying an unspoken summons from the painted figure itself.

He was drawn to the portrait, unable to resist its captivating allure. Emotions swirled within him, threatening to break his stoic facade. His hand twitched, longing to touch and feel the intense energy emanating from the painting's lines and curves.

"Blimey," he murmured, his voice a hushed rasp of awe and reverence. "It's as if the bloody thing's alive."

In that instant, Alex was captivated and lost all self-control as he succumbed to the raw power of the artwork. It was a shock to his system, unveiling buried emotions and disrupting the carefully crafted facade he had maintained for so long.

"What do you see, mate?" a voice inquired from beside him, startling Alex from his reverie.

He turned to find a fellow patron regarding him with a knowing smile, their gaze following the trajectory of Alex's fixation upon the portrait.

Clearing his throat, Alex struggled to regain his customary poise, his fingers absently tugging at the cuff of his impeccably tailored shirt. "A masterful command of technique, to be sure," he replied, his words laced with the faintest tremor of vulnerability. "But more than that...a raw, unfettered expression of the artist's spirit. It's quite..."

He hesitated, unaccustomed to unveiling the depths of his inner turmoil, even in the presence of a stranger. Yet, the portrait had awakened something primal within him, a longing to shed the confines of his rigid control and simply...feel.

"Bloody brilliant," Alex concluded, the corners of his lips curving ever so slightly upward in a rare, unguarded smile.

Alex gave a curt nod to the stranger, dismissing their company as his gaze returned to the magnetic pull of the portrait. He could feel the weight of its unspoken truth bearing down upon him, challenging the meticulously constructed facade he so skillfully maintained.

With a sharp exhale, Alex turned on his heel and strode towards the courtyard, his polished oxfords echoing against the marble floor. He needed air, space to breathe and collect the fragments of his composure that threatened to unravel.

The heavy oak door yielded beneath his palm, and Alex stepped out into the tranquil oasis of the courtyard. A gentle breeze caressed his face, carrying the faint scent of jasmine and offering a fleeting respite from the oppressive intensity of the exhibit.

Unbuttoning his suit jacket, Alex allowed himself to sink onto a wrought-iron bench, his fingers instinctively loosening the knot of his tie. This small act of vulnerability felt strangely liberating, a momentary surrender to the turmoil that simmered beneath his impeccable veneer.

As he leaned back, his gaze drifted skyward, finding solace in the vast expanse of the evening sky. The setting sun painted the heavens in a kaleidoscope of colors, a breathtaking canvas that stirred something deep within his soul.

In moments of solitude, Alex faced his inner demons. The constant desire for control and fear of losing it kept him from appreciating the beauty around him.

A soft footfall on the cobblestones drew Alex's attention, and he turned to find a young woman regarding him with a curious tilt of her head. Her wild, tousled curls and paint-splattered overalls marked her as one of the exhibiting artists, a stark contrast to Alex's polished appearance.

"You seem troubled," she observed, her voice carrying a gentle lilt that betrayed her artistic sensibilities.

Alex arched a brow, his defenses instinctively rising in the face of such blatant scrutiny. "I assure you, I'm quite alright," he replied, his tone clipped and dismissive.

Yet, the artist remained undeterred, her gaze holding his with an intensity that belied her unassuming demeanor. "Art has a way of stirring the soul, am I right?" she mused, taking a step closer. "Of revealing the truths we so desperately strive to conceal, even from ourselves."

A muscle twitched in Alex's jaw as her words struck a chord within him, resonating with the very conflict that had driven him to seek refuge in this secluded sanctuary. Before he could formulate a retort, the artist continued, her voice laden with a wisdom that seemed to defy her youthful appearance.

"Perhaps it is not control that you crave, but rather the illusion of it – a shield against the raw, unbridled essence of life that threatens to unravel the carefully curated existence you've so meticulously constructed."

Alex's breath caught in his throat, his defenses crumbling under the weight of her profound insight. It was as if she had peered into the depths of his soul, laying bare the very demons he had spent a lifetime concealing.

He was faced with a decision: remain guarded or open himself up to vulnerability, potentially leading to a more genuine life.

The words that tumbled from his lips surprised even himself, a raw, unguarded admission that shattered the boundaries he had so carefully maintained. "How does one let go?"

The artist regarded him with a knowing smile, her eyes sparkling with the wisdom of one who had traversed the path he now found himself upon. "By surrendering to the beauty of the present moment, without expectation or judgment. By allowing the ebb and flow of life to carry you, rather than attempting to impose your will upon it."

As she spoke, Alex felt a deep change within him. He realized that true freedom wasn't about controlling everything, but rather the brave act of letting go and surrendering. It was terrifying, yet exhilarating.

Alex took a deep breath and returned his attention to the exhibit. He slowly observed each artwork, letting go of his critical analysis and allowing himself to be fully immersed in the experience. The vibrant colors, bold strokes, and raw emotions of the artists spoke to him in a way he had never experienced before. It was a transformation, a release from the rigid constraints of his previous mindset. As time passed, he felt the weight of expectations and control fade, replaced by a genuine appreciation for the imperfect yet beautiful art around him.

Lost in the complexity of a captivating painting, Alex's attention was drawn to a rebellious brushstroke. He chuckled at its unapologetic imperfection, realizing that true art lies in raw expression rather than perfection.

As the exhibition ended, Alex felt a newfound sense of wonder and possibility. No longer confined by self-imposed boundaries, he embraced life's messy complexities. This experience would shape his perspective and lead him on a journey of self-discovery.

three

The dimly lit interior of Mo's Jazz Club enveloped Alex in a smoky haze as he stepped through the door. His eyes slowly adjusted, scanning the intimate space teeming with an eclectic array of patrons—some swaying to the sultry melodies, others engaged in hushed conversations over half-empty glasses. With a discerning gaze, he sought an unoccupied table, one that would afford him an unobstructed view of the stage.

"Evenin', Mr. Shefton," Mo's booming baritone resonated from across the room, cutting through the melodic discord. "Your usual spot's open."

Alex offered a curt nod of acknowledgment, weaving his way through the cluster of bodies. The pungent aroma of cigarette smoke mingled with the earthy notes of whiskey, creating an intoxicating blend that seemed to seep into the very fabric of the establishment. As he settled into the plush crimson seat, the remnants of a woman's perfume lingered—a heady, musky scent that stirred something primal within him.

The stage lights illuminated the performer's face, casting shadows and highlighting their emotion as they played the guitar with skillful fingers. Alex sat back, fully immersed in the soulful music that resonated within him.

"What'll it be?" The waitress, a petite redhead adorned with a coquettish smile, materialized at his side, notepad in hand.

"Macallan, neat," Alex replied without sparing her a glance, his attention fixated on the stage.

He took a swig of alcohol, feeling its fiery burn down his throat. He was entranced by the intense emotion pouring out from the musicians, every note resonating within him. In these moments, surrounded by chaos and the smell of vice, he felt alive and free from the controlled life he had constructed for himself.

The sultry melody faded, and a hush fell over the dimly lit club as the performer took a bow, their exit met with thunderous applause. Alex joined in the ovation, his hands meeting with a measured cadence, his gaze already shifting towards the stage in anticipation of what was to come.

A solitary spotlight pierced through the hazy atmosphere, its beam trained upon the sleek, polished form of a cello that stood proudly at the center of the stage. Alex felt his pulse quicken as a figure emerged from the wings, her stride exuding a quiet confidence that commanded the room's attention.

The African-American woman was a striking figure in her black-red laced corset over a long red skirt, accentuating her curves. Her dark curls framed a face with defined cheekbones and full lips, but it was her amber eyes that caught Alex's attention. They held an intensity that contradicted her calm appearance.

With a practiced grace, the woman settled upon the stool, her fingers caressing the polished wood of the cello's neck as one would a lover. A heavy silence hung in the air, charged with anticipation, until finally, she drew the bow across the strings in one fluid motion.

Alex was taken aback by the unexpected sound of *"Le cygne"* in a jazz club. The classical piece, played with such elegance and grace by a stunning musician, seemed out of place amidst the lively atmosphere. He couldn't help but be captivated by the beautiful melody that filled the room, transporting him to another world. His initial surprise gave way to admiration and he found himself drawn to the performer on stage, marveling at her talent and presence. It was a moment he would never forget, the collision of two different genres creating an unforgettable experience.

The first few notes resounded through the intimate space, rich and resonant, like the beating of a powerful heart. Alex found himself leaning forward, his elbows resting upon the table as he surrendered himself to the ebb and flow of the woman's impassioned performance.

Her brow furrowed in concentration, every muscle taut with the exertion of channeling the raw emotion that poured forth from her instrument. Each swell, each crescendo, seemed to tear away at the fragile veil separating them from the tempestuous depths of her soul.

Alex was transfixed, his gaze drinking in the sight of her fingers dancing across the strings with a deftness that bordered on reverence. In that moment, she was equal parts siren and maestro, weaving an intoxicating tapestry of sound that threatened to unravel the very threads of his composure.

The last note hung in the air, and Alex held his breath, not wanting to interrupt the intensity of the moment. Only when thunderous applause broke through did he remember to breathe again, his chest rising and falling with the weight of what had just happened.

The woman's eyes fluttered open, and for a fleeting moment, her gaze locked with Alex's. In that instant, an unspoken connection sparked between them, a wordless acknowledgment of the profound journey they had just shared through her music.

Alex felt a strange stirring within him, a hunger ignited by the raw vulnerability she had laid bare before him. It was as if she had stripped away the veneer of his cultured existence, exposing the primal yearnings that lay dormant beneath the surface.

As the applause gradually subsided, Alex found himself rising to his feet, compelled by an inexplicable force that propelled him towards the shadowed recesses of the backstage area. He *had* to meet her, to bask in her presence and unravel the enigma that had so utterly captivated him.

As he walked, his interest grew, reminding him of her passionate performance. The echoes of her music lingered in his body, a tempting beat that drowned out his logical thoughts.

As Alex drew nearer to the backstage area, his heart thundered in his chest, a discordant counterpoint to the lingering strains of the woman's playing that still echoed in his mind. He could scarcely comprehend the intensity of his reaction, this overwhelming desire to be in her presence, to bask in the radiance of her talent.

The dim corridor opened into a small lounge area, where a handful of performers milled about, still buzzing with the adrenaline of their performances. Alex's gaze swept the room, searching, until finally, it settled upon her.

The woman stood with her back to him, engaged in conversation with a couple of stagehands. Even from behind, her regal bearing was unmistakable, the curve of her neck arching with a grace that stirred something primal within him.

As if sensing his scrutiny, she turned, and their eyes met in an electric instant that seemed to suspend time itself. Her expressive eyes, still smoldering with the remnants of her impassioned performance, locked onto his with an intensity that threatened to consume him.

They shared a silent moment, their connection evident in the way her music had moved him. Alex couldn't look away from her captivating gaze, feeling overwhelmed by a mix of admiration, curiosity, and an undeniable attraction to her.

He was at the mercy of his desire, unable to resist the pull he felt towards the woman. Her very presence demanded his attention, and every small movement she made stirred something deep within him that he struggled to understand or contain.

With a subtle tilt of her head, she regarded him curiously, those eyes seeming to penetrate the very core of his being. And in that instant, Alex knew he was lost, ensnared by the allure of this extraordinary woman and the promise of a connection that threatened to upend the carefully curated existence he had so meticulously constructed.

Without a second thought, he approached her, his footsteps muffled by the plush carpet beneath his feet. "Excuse me," he began, his voice rich and cultured, a product of his privileged upbringing.

The woman turned slowly, her dark eyes regarding him with a guarded curiosity. Up close, Alex could see the faint sheen of perspiration that glistened across her brow, a testament to the intensity of her art. "Yes?" she replied, her tone cautious yet laced with a hint of intrigue.

Alex offered her a disarming smile, one that had charmed countless patrons and critics alike. "Please, allow me to introduce myself. Alexander Shefton, art connoisseur and unabashed admirer of your extraordinary talent."

A flicker of recognition passed across the woman's features, her full lips curving into a tentative smile. "We have the same name," she giggled.

Alex was warmed by her smile alone, "Your name is Alexander too?"

She held out her hand to him and shook his, "Priscilla *Alexander*," she purred, "but my friends call me, Prissy."

Alex gave her a roguish grin, "So nice to make your acquaintance, Prissy."

Prissy dropped her eyes down the length of him. *Tall and good-looking, brown hair, green eyes, white-guy-frat-boy, if it weren't for his accent.* "You're the one they call the 'Curator's *Curator*,' aren't you? I've heard whispers about your keen eye for undiscovered brilliance."

"Guilty as charged," Alex chuckled, his gaze roaming over her face, committing every nuance to memory. "But tonight, it was your brilliance that consumed me utterly. Your mastery of the cello, the raw emotion you poured into every note..." He trailed off, shaking his head in wonder. "It was a transcendent experience, one that left me quite breathless."

Prissy's eyes narrowed ever so slightly, her expression inscrutable. "High praise, indeed. And from such an esteemed critic, no less."

"Merely an honest assessment from one who appreciates true artistry," Alex countered smoothly. "Tell me, Miss Alexander, what drives your passion? What inspires the depth of feeling you imbue into your music?"

For a moment, Prissy seemed to study him, her gaze probing and assessing. Then, almost imperceptibly, the tension in her shoulders eased, and she favored him with a slow, enigmatic smile. "Why don't you allow me to show you?"

Alex arched an inquisitive brow, his interest piqued by her provocative invitation. "I would be delighted."

Prissy's smile deepened, a sensual curve of her lips that hinted at mysteries yet unrevealed. "Very well, then." Without another word, she turned and headed deeper into the shadowed recesses of the backstage area.

Intrigued, Alex followed, his long strides carrying him through the dimly lit corridor. The muted sounds of the club faded into the distance, replaced by the soft tapping of Prissy's heels against the concrete floor. At last, she paused before an unmarked door, glancing back at him over her shoulder with a look that bordered on challenge.

"In here," she murmured, pushing the door open to reveal a small, sparse room. A single chair sat in the center, facing a desk cluttered with sheet music and well-worn notebooks.

Alex entered the room and Prissy immediately moved to her chair. She sat down with a calm ease, but there was an underlying intensity in her demeanor. She picked up her cello, holding it with a gentle touch that hinted at a strong emotional connection.

"This is where the magic happens," she said, her voice a low, throaty purr. "Where I seek solace from the world and lose myself in the language of emotion." Her fingers caressed the strings, coaxing forth a rich, resonant hum that seemed to reverberate through Alex's very core.

He found himself holding his breath, captivated by the sight of her—this magnificent creature who channeled her very essence into her art. Prissy's eyes drifted shut, her lashes casting delicate shadows across her cheekbones as she began to play.

The initial notes were unsure, as if feeling out the room. But as the music continued, it grew in strength and intensity. Prissy's body moved with a fluid sensuality, a primitive dance in harmony with the building sound.

Alex was drowning, utterly consumed by the raw power of her performance. It was as if Prissy had reached into the depths of his soul, laying bare every desire, every longing he'd ever experienced. His grip tightened on the back of the chair before him, knuckles whitening as he struggled to maintain his composure.

When at last the final, quivering note dissipated into silence, Alex found himself trembling, his chest heaving with the force of emotion that gripped him. Prissy's eyes fluttered open, meeting his with an intensity that threatened to shatter his carefully cultivated restraint.

"That..." He swallowed hard, his voice emerging as a ragged whisper. "That was breathtaking."

A slow, knowing smile curved Prissy's lips. "I'm glad you appreciated the performance, Mr. Shefton." She rose from the chair, closing the distance between them with predatory grace. "Because I have a proposition for you."

Alex could only stare, mesmerized by her proximity, the scent of her filling his senses. "A proposition?" he managed, his tone edged with a husky rawness.

"Yes." Prissy's gaze held his, bold and unwavering. "I want you to feature me in your next exhibition. Give me a chance to showcase my talents on an international stage."

For a heartbeat, Alex was rendered speechless, stunned by the audacity of her request. Then, gradually, a slow smile curved his lips—a smile tinged with appreciation and a hint of something far more primal.

"Miss Alexander," he purred, leaning in until his lips were a hairsbreadth from her ear. "It would be my distinct honor and pleasure."

four

"Would you care to join me for a walk, Miss Alexander?" Alex coaxed, his gentle voice laced with charm and sincerity. He held out his hand to her, hoping she would follow. "We can continue discussing your proposition and get to know each other better."

Prissy regarded the man before her, taking in every detail of his aristocratic features and confident stance. Despite his obvious wealth and privileged upbringing, there was something intriguing about him that drew her in. She couldn't deny the hint of attraction flickering within her.

With a slight hesitation, Prissy finally gave him a small smile and placed her hand in his. "I suppose a walk wouldn't hurt."

Leaving behind the bustling crowds of people, they strolled through the cool evening air and basked in the soft glow of the moonlight. As they walked side by side, they delved into deeper conversations and satisfied their curiosity about one another's pasts and aspirations. The night seemed to stretch on endlessly as they lost track of time engrossed in each other's company.

"You were...captivating up there. Quite electrifying, really." He said, shoving his hands down his pant pockets.

Prissy arched one eyebrow. "I aim to move people with my music. Though I'm surprised a high society art snob could detect any soul in it."

The words dripped from his lips like honey, each one laced with a hint of mischief. His lupine smile tugged at the corner of his mouth, beckoning her into his game. "Ah, the assumption that my privileged upbringing deadened all capacity for genuine feeling," he chuckled, his eyes sparkling with amusement.

Prissy raised an eyebrow, unimpressed by his coy demeanor. "Where are you from?"

He played along, drawing out the game a little longer. "Oh, just a little place called England," he said in a teasing tone.

Rolling her eyes, Prissy couldn't help but feel a twinge of annoyance at his vague answer. "Yes, by your accent I assumed that. But from where exactly?"

"Manchester," Alex finally admitted, looking down at his shoes as if suddenly ashamed of his hometown. The air around them seemed to shift, as if clouded by memories or regrets.

Prissy leaned forward, her eyes sparkling with mischief as she asked, "And do you call this place home forever? Or is it just for the sake of art?" Alex's lips curled into a half-smile at her teasing tone, mirroring the way she was toying with him.

"I've been fortunate enough to call California my home for almost five years," he admitted proudly. His gaze drifted to the distant horizon, filled with warm memories of his time here. "But I always make sure to fly back every Christmas, no matter where life takes me."

Her gaze narrowed skeptically even as she felt an unmistakable charge low in her abdomen from his smoldering inspection. The arrogance was insufferable, but something about the predatory glint in his eyes made her thighs instinctively press together.

Prissy came to a halt, her feet sinking into the soft brick wall as she sat down gingerly. She looked up at the man standing before her, his chiseled features and green eyes making him look almost inhumanly perfect. For a moment, she couldn't help but admire him, despite her better judgment. His gaze was hungry and intense, causing her to feel vulnerable and exposed under its weight. Every inch of her body felt like it was being scrutinized by his piercing stare.

"Your passion resonates," Alex murmured, taking a bold step closer. The sandalwood cologne enveloping him was as rich as his cultured cadence. "The way you lose yourself in the music, surrendering every fiber of your being..." His voice lowered an octave. "It's utterly spellbinding."

A shiver rippled through Prissy at his words. She found herself equal parts flustered and intrigued by his unabashed forwardness. "You have a...distinctive way with compliments, Mr. Shefton."

"Merely giving credit where it's due." Alex's penetrating stare held hers captive. "I'd be honored if you'd allow me to take you for a drink sometime. To discuss artistry and...other enthralling topics."

Was he flirting with her? The blatant undercurrent of his invitation hung thick between them. Prissy's chest tightened as unbidden thoughts drifted to how his sophisticated hands might feel tracing the curves she normally kept hidden beneath her conservative attire.

Drawing a steadying breath, she cocked her head. "Is that your customary way of propositioning women? Tossing out grandiose flattery dipped in innuendo?"

"Only with the rare few who inspire such...admiration." The right corner of his mouth curved upward with devastating charm. "I simply call it as I see it, love. No bewilderment required."

Prissy's cheeks warmed at both the endearment and his brazen desire. This man didn't just ooze wealth - he oozed an entitled arrogance she found simultaneously infuriating and arousing. *Perhaps a drink would be...educational.*

Prissy eyed Alex appraisingly, taking in his impeccably tailored suit and air of effortless sophistication. A stark contrast to her own off-the-shoulder dress, its vibrant patterns a subtle nod to her African heritage. She thought about her proposition earlier, the whole reason she agreed to take a walk with this *British Casanova.*

"Very well, Mr. Shefton." She smoothed a hand over the glossy curls spilling past her shoulders. "One drink couldn't hurt, I suppose. Though I can't guarantee I'll prove quite the...enthralling companion you seem to envision."

A delighted grin split his chiseled features. "Bollocks. With a woman of your incredible talent and refined sensibilities? I have no doubt you'll be a riveting conversationalist."

As Alex gestured back toward the jazz club, Prissy couldn't resist a teasing jab. "For someone dripping in British propriety, you certainly don't mince words, do you?"

"Ah, but where would be the fun in that?" He slanted her a roguish look as they walked. "I find candor to be the specter of scoundrels and poets alike. We sophisticated sorts mustn't be afraid to give voice to our...adventurous appetites on occasion."

Prissy's breath hitched at the undisguised heat shadowing his gaze. *Just what sort of appetites was this man implying?* A shiver of delighted trepidation ran through her. Whatever game he was playing at, she found herself inexplicably tempted to play along. *At least for tonight.*

"Is that so? Then do enlighten me, Mr. Shefton. What sort of...indulgences do sophisticates like us partake in?" She couldn't deny the spark of heat kindling low in her belly at the charged tension crackling between them. This was new territory for the usually reserved musician - brazenly flirting with a virtual stranger. But there was something about this cultured Englishman that called to her wild side in a way she couldn't resist.

Alex leveled a searing look at her from beneath hooded lids as he leaned in harmfully. "Where to begin?" His voice dropped to a low rumble that sent a shiver down her spine. "Pursuits of the mind and body, I'd wager. The finest vintners and cuisines the world has to offer. Reveling in the raw passion of the arts - music, painting, dance..."

His heated gaze raked over her appreciatively. "Luxuriating in beauty in all its forms. Wherever it may be found."

A blush stole into Prissy's cheeks at his blatant appraisal. Heat unfurled through her core as she wondered just how far this man's definition of 'beauty' extended.

Forcing a casual tone, she arched one elegant brow. "My, my. A life of wanton hedonism, is it? I must admit, you've piqued my curiosity about these...indulgences." She traced the rim of her glass with one fingertip. "Care to elaborate?"

The corner of Alex's sculptured mouth kicked up. "Gladly. Though actions, I find, convey such...intrigues far better than words."

His stormy gaze held her transfixed as he closed the scant distance between them. Prissy's breath caught as his large, calloused hand cupped her chin with exquisite gentleness, tilting her face up to his.

"Allow me to provide a small...demonstration," he murmured darkly.

Then his mouth was on hers - a searing brand of velvet heat and dizzying skill that robbed Prissy of all coherent thought.

Alex's kiss was like a raging wildfire, consuming Prissy with its scorching intensity. His lips moved against hers with an urgency that belied the confident control in his touch, as if he were a man starved for her taste.

Prissy surrendered to his intense embrace, her doubts fading away as their burning desire overtook them both. Her hands gripped his jacket tightly, pulling him closer as she matched his fervor.

When the need for air finally forced them apart, Alex's eyes glittered like smoldering coals in their heated appraisal of her flushed, kiss-swollen lips. "Exquisite," he rasped in a low rumble of pure sin.

Prissy struggled to catch her breath, her body still buzzing from the intense kiss she had just shared with this suave and alluring man. But as the excitement settled, her old defense mechanism kicked in - a reminder to protect herself from any potential heartbreak. She fidgeted with her hair, an uncharacteristically shy gesture for her.

"You're quite the alluring troublemaker, Mr. Shefton," she said, trying to regain her composure. "But just so you know, I'm not easily swayed into improper behavior."

The wolfish glint in Alex's eyes spoke volumes of his opinion on such matters of propriety. "A wise man knows better than to make assumptions about a woman's...appetites," he rumbled silkily. "Especially one as full of surprises as yourself, Miss Alexander."

His fingertips trailed lightly down the curve of her cheek in a scorching caress. "I look forward to unraveling each and every one of your mysteries."

The dimly lit backstage area had nearly emptied, leaving Prissy and Alex in a cocoon of hushed intimacy. Yet their voices rose and fell with spirited animation, fueled by the raw passion burgeoning between them.

"Art speaks to the soul in a way mere words cannot," Prissy insisted, her eyes alight with fervor. "When I play, I bare the depths of my emotions - the soaring heights of joy, the aching hollows of sorrow. It transcends the physical realm."

Alex leaned in, utterly transfixed by the impassioned cadence of her voice. "You play as if possessed by some higher muse, darling. As if the music itself flows through your very veins." His words caressed her skin like a phantom touch.

A faint flush stained Prissy's cheeks at such unabashed

admiration. "You give me far too much credit, Mr. Shefton. I am but a conduit for the sublime beauty that music can evoke."

"Ah, but therein lies the true artistry!" Alex's eyes danced with delight at her modesty. "To channel such raw emotion and render it into something that stirs the very fabric of one's being - that is a rare gift indeed."

Their eyes met, fiery with longing and a sense of familiarity. Everything else faded away in that moment, leaving only the two of them - connected by an intangible bond of understanding and desire.

"Do you feel it?" Prissy murmured, her lush lips parting on a tremulous breath. "This...energy between us?"

A low rumble of laughter escaped Alex as he boldly bridged the space between them. "Like a live wire thrumming beneath my skin, love." His fingertips ghosted along the curve of her jaw as his voice lowered to a husky rasp. "I've never felt more alive."

The charged air thickened around them as Alex's hand lingered against Prissy's cheek, his touch feather-light yet scorching in its intensity. Prissy's pulse fluttered wildly beneath her skin as she found herself utterly enraptured by this sophisticated stranger.

"Will you tell me more about this exhibition you mentioned earlier?" Prissy asked, leaning away from him now.

Alex cleared his throat, "Yes, of course. Will you meet me tomorrow? At my office downtown?"

A discreet cough from the nearby stage manager shattered the delicious tension. "Miss Alexander? We're needing to clear out the backstage now."

Prissy blinked, jolted back to awareness of their surroundings. The once-bustling area was now nearly deserted, leaving her and Alex as the sole occupants caught in the intimate pocket they'd inadvertently created.

Reluctance warred with propriety until she managed a small nod. "Of course. My apologies."

She struggled to look away from Alex's intense gaze. They exchanged contact information, their fingers barely touching as they made plans and left unanswered questions hanging in the air. A jumble of excitement and unease swirled inside her.

"See you later, Mr. Shefton," Prissy said in a low, sultry voice.

Alex's lips curved into a rakish grin as he brushed a courtly kiss across her knuckles. "I shall count the moments, my dear."

Prissy walked out of the backstage area and took a moment to catch her breath. She leaned against the hallway wall, trying to calm the racing of her heart. *What exactly had just happened between her and the mysterious Englishman?* The memory of his touch still lingered on her skin, proof of the undeniable chemistry they shared as artists.

She held onto Alex's number tightly in her hand, torn between excitement and fear. *Was she ready to take a chance with him? Or would it only lead to trouble in the long run?* The possibilities were both alluring and dangerous.

Taking a deep breath, Prissy pushed aside her doubts. Their meeting tonight had changed everything, for better or worse. They were now connected by something magical, known only to those who are truly touched by their muse's call.

Alex stood still in the thinning crowd, watching as Prissy walked away and turned the corner. A small smile appeared on his face as he shook his head, trying to make sense of the mix of strength and fragility that he had seen in her tonight.

"Well, well..." he murmured under his breath, shoving his hands into the pockets of his impeccably-tailored trousers. "Wasn't quite expecting all that, eh?"

The echoes of her impassioned performance still seemed to reverberate through his very core. Like a maelstrom of emotion given hauntingly beautiful, visceral form through the lush lamentations of her cello. In that moment, she had utterly captivated him - mind, body, and soul enraptured by the unbridled intensity simmering beneath her regal facade.

He huffed out a low chuckle tinged with self-deprecation. *Leave it to you to get tangled up with another bloody complicated one, Al.*

He couldn't pretend to be surprised. His relationships were always complicated - a dance of power and temptation hidden beneath the facade of sophistication. It was a game he had mastered through years of mingling with the elite in high society.

But there was something unique about Prissy Alexander. Something that sparked an unknown desire - a need - to uncover the raw truth hidden beneath her intense demeanor. To break through the barriers around her heart and experience the unbridled emotions trapped within.

A shiver of anticipation rippled through him as he palmed the slim card bearing her number. The thrill of the hunt was undeniable...and all the more enticing for the lofty challenge she presented.

Yes, he would pursue this delicious enigma of a woman. Mercilessly. Relentlessly. He would carefully peeled back every layer of her until he claimed her heart as his own.

five

Prissy drummed her crimson nails against the café's worn oak table, a torrent of nervous energy coursing through her veins. The scent of fresh espresso mingled with the soft murmurs of the café's patrons, creating a cozy symphony that did little to soothe her restless mind.

The tinkling of the bell above the door grabbed her attention, and there was Miriam, a beacon of warmth amidst the bustling café. Her radiant smile lit up the room as their eyes met, and Prissy felt a wave of relief wash over her.

"Girl, you made it!" Prissy exclaimed, rising from her seat as Miriam enveloped her in a tight embrace. Her sister's familiar warmth enveloped her, a temporary reprieve from the storm of emotions raging within.

Miriam had been more than just a guardian to Prissy ever since they lost their biological mother to cancer when Prissy was just four years old. At the time, Miriam was only eighteen herself, but she took on the role of caregiver with unwavering determination. She worked tirelessly to help elevate Prissy's career and give her every opportunity in life. To Prissy, Miriam was not just a mentor or a protector, but a true mother figure who had sacrificed everything for her well-being. And as she stood on the cusp of success, Prissy knew that she owed it all to Miriam's love and guidance throughout the years.

"Of course, sis. You know I'd never miss a chance to see that beautiful face of yours," Miriam replied, her voice rich with affection as she held Prissy close, silently conveying her unwavering support.

Prissy melted into the embrace, savoring the comfort of her sister's presence. For a fleeting moment, the world around her seemed to fade away, leaving only the two of them in their own little sanctuary.

Prissy reluctantly pulled away from the embrace, a heavy sigh escaping her lips as she sank back into her chair. "Thanks for coming, sis. I really need to talk to you about somethin'."

Miriam's gentle gaze met Prissy's, her expression a perfect blend of patience and understanding. "Of course, sweetie. You know I'm all ears."

Prissy's fingers fidgeted with the edge of the worn tablecloth, her mind racing as she tried to find the right words. "You know that fancy British art guy, Alex? Well, he came to one of my shows the other night and... damn, sis, he was blown away."

A glimmer of excitement flickered in Miriam's eyes, but she remained silent, allowing Prissy to continue at her own pace.

"He wants to sign me to some big art exhibition," Prissy confessed, her voice laced with a mixture of awe and apprehension. "Said he could make me a star, help me take my music to the next level."

Prissy's gaze drifted to the steaming cup of coffee before her, her expression clouded with doubt. "I don't know what to do, Miriam. This could be huge for my career, but... I'm scared, you know? Scared of what it might mean, of stepping outside my comfort zone." Her fingers drummed against the table once more, a nervous tic that betrayed the turmoil brewing beneath the surface. "And if I'm being real honest here... there's something about Alex that just... draws me in, you feel me?" Leaning forward, Prissy's voice lowered to a conspiratorial whisper. "I can't stop thinking about him, sis. It's like he's got me under some kinda spell or something."

Miriam reached across the table, her warm hand enveloping Prissy's fidgeting fingers. Her touch was gentle, grounding, a silent reassurance that she was there, listening without judgment.

"Sweetie, it's okay to be scared," Miriam soothed, her voice a calming balm against Prissy's frayed nerves. "Change can be terrifying, but it can also be the start of something incredible."

Prissy's eyes welled up with tears as she admitted her deepest fear. "I'm scared of losing myself, you know? What if this opportunity with Alex changes me, makes me someone I don't even recognize?" She swallowed hard, blinking back the moisture threatening to spill down her cheeks. "And what about Rafe? We got something special, me and him. If I go down this path with Alex, what's gonna happen to us? I don't wanna lose that connection we got."

Miriam's heart ached for her sister, her own experiences echoing through Prissy's words. She gave Prissy's hand a reassuring squeeze, drawing her in with a tender gaze.

"Honey, I know it's scary, but the truth is, change is inevitable. We either embrace it or let it pass us by." Miriam paused, gathering her thoughts. "It's true, Rafe found you your gig at Mo's Jazz Club, but you were always meant for bigger and better things."

Prissy listened to her sister whole-heartedly. "I'm afraid to hurt him."

Leaning back, Miriam's eyes took on a faraway look, a wistful smile playing on her lips. "Remember when I quit my job at the firm to start that nonprofit? Everyone thought I was crazy, but Marcus supported me every step of the way. He believed in me, even when I didn't believe in myself." She refocused on Prissy, her expression earnest. "Taking risks is never easy, but it's how we evolve, how we find our true path. And as for Rafe, he'll understand. You were *always* meant for the heavens, Priss. You just gotta have faith, baby girl."

Prissy took a deep, steadying breath, letting Miriam's words wash over her. She could feel the tension in her shoulders ebbing away, replaced by a newfound clarity. Her sister was right – she didn't have to sacrifice one passion for another. There had to be a way to embrace both her music and this unexpected connection with Alex.

Miriam leaned forward, her gaze unwavering. "Listen, I know you got a lotta questions swirlin' around in that beautiful head of yours. So why don't you sit down with Alex again, lay it all out on the table? Have an honest conversation about your concerns, your dreams, everything. Explore the possibilities together."

She reached across the table, giving Prissy's hand a reassuring squeeze. "Life's too damn short to let fear call the shots, Priss. You gotta take that leap, even when the landing ain't all mapped out."

Prissy's eyes flickered with a mix of trepidation and determination. Miriam was right – she owed it to herself to at least hear Alex out, to understand what this opportunity could mean for her career, for her life. Maybe he had some insight, some perspective that could help ease her doubts.

"Ok, you made your point," Prissy conceded with a wry smile, her fingers curling around Miriam's hand in a silent gesture of gratitude. "I'll hit him up, see if we can talk it through. No harm in keeping an open mind, right?"

Miriam's face lit up with a proud grin. "That's my girl! Just promise me one thing – whatever you decide, make sure it's what you *really* want, not what anyone else expects of you. This is your life, Priss. You gotta live it on your own terms."

As Prissy nodded, a newfound sense of purpose thrummed within her. For too long, she'd allowed fear to dictate her choices, to keep her confined within the boundaries of her comfort zone. But now, with Miriam's unwavering support, she felt ready to step into the unknown, to embrace whatever possibilities awaited her – even if it meant navigating uncharted territory.

Miriam leaned back in her chair, basking in the warmth of Prissy's resolve. "I know you got this, sis. You're one talented lady, and the world deserves to hear what you have to say – with your music and your spirit."

A wistful smile tugged at the corners of Prissy's lips as she pondered Miriam's words. Her sister had an uncanny ability to cut through the noise, to strip away the layers of self-doubt and insecurity that so often weighed Prissy down. With Miriam in her corner, she felt like she could conquer any obstacle, face down any fear that threatened to hold her back.

"Yeah, you right," Prissy murmured, her fingers absently tracing the rim of her coffee cup. "Time to stop playin' it safe and really put myself out there, consequences be damned." A determined glint flickered in her deep brown eyes as she met Miriam's gaze.

Miriam reached across the table, giving Prissy's hand an affectionate squeeze. "That's my girl. Just remember, whatever happens, I got your back. You ain't gotta go through this alone, you hear me?"

A grateful smile spread across Prissy's face as she returned the gesture, reveling in the unwavering bond she shared with her sister. With Miriam by her side, she felt invincible – like she could take on the world and come out on top, no matter what challenges lay ahead.

As they rose to leave the cozy café, Prissy couldn't help but feel a sense of excited trepidation coursing through her veins. This was it – the moment she'd been both dreading and anticipating, the crossroads where her life could veer in an entirely new direction. But for once, the fear didn't paralyze her; instead, it ignited a fire within, a fierce determination to seize control of her destiny and forge her own path, consequences be damned.

Prissy emerged from the café into the crisp evening air, the sounds of the bustling city enveloping her as she and Miriam strolled down the sidewalk. A gentle breeze tousled her dark curls, carrying with it the faint aroma of blooming flowers from a nearby park. Despite the chaos swirling around them, Prissy felt a newfound sense of clarity, as if the weight of her indecision had been lifted from her shoulders.

"Thanks for real, sis," she said, looping her arm through Miriam's as they walked. "I don't know what I'd do without you keepin' it real with me."

Miriam chuckled, her warm smile crinkling the corners of her eyes. "Girl, you know I got you. Just promise me you'll take care of yourself, a'ight? Don't let this Alex dude pull you too far off your path."

Prissy nodded, her expression sobering. "I feel you. I'm gonna keep it a hundred with him, lay it all out on the table. If he can't respect my talent and who I am, then it ain't meant to be."

As they approached the intersection where their paths would diverge, Prissy pulled Miriam into a tight embrace. "Love you, sis."

"Love you too, Priss. Now go get 'em, tiger." Miriam gave her a playful wink before turning and heading off down the street, leaving Prissy to navigate the next steps of her journey alone.

With a deep breath, Prissy reached into her bag and retrieved her phone, her thumb hovering over the screen as she debated her next move. Finally, she tapped out a message to Alex, her heart pounding in her chest.

> Hey, it's Prissy Alexander. You free to meet up and talk about that opportunity? Let me know when works for you.

She hit send before she could second-guess herself, and

almost immediately, the three dots appeared, indicating that Alex was typing a response. Prissy's stomach twisted into anxious knots as she waited, her mind racing with a whirlwind of possibilities.

The reply from Alex came swiftly, his words carrying an unmistakable enthusiasm that both thrilled and unnerved Prissy.

> Priscilla, delighted to hear from you. Your eagerness is most welcome. I would be honored to discuss this endeavor further at my gallery tomorrow, say, 3 o'clock? Address is on the card. I shall make the necessary arrangements to ensure we shan't be disturbed.

Prissy read the message twice, her brow furrowing at the formality of his phrasing. She could practically hear the clipped, posh British accent in her mind, a stark contrast to her own urban cadence. With a slight shake of her head, she typed out a response.

> See you then

She stuffed her phone back into her bag, a nervous energy coursing through her veins. Glancing at her watch, she realized she had several hours to burn before her gig started at Mo's. Knowing idle hands would only fuel her anxieties, Prissy made her way home, her strides purposeful.

Once inside her modest apartment, she wasted no time in retrieving her beloved cello from its case. The rich, polished wood seemed to glow in the filtered sunlight, beckoning her with its promise of solace. Prissy settled onto the well-worn sofa, cradling the instrument against her body like an old friend.

With a deep, steadying breath, she drew the bow across the strings, the first few notes emerging tentative and uncertain. But as the music swelled around her, Prissy allowed the melodies to carry her worries away, pouring every ounce of her turbulent emotions into the resonant vibrations.

The cello became an extension of her very soul, each plaintive note a confession, a desperate plea for understanding. Prissy lost herself in the push and pull of the melancholic refrains, her brow furrowed in intense focus, beads of perspiration forming along her hairline.

As the last notes faded away, Prissy felt a sense of calm wash over her. Her turbulent thoughts calmed down and she felt determined. She was Priscilla Alexander, not to be underestimated. She would confront this opportunity - and Alex - on her own terms.

With a resolute nod, she gently returned the cello to its case and rose to her feet, stretching her taut muscles. The path ahead might be fraught with uncertainty, but Prissy knew she possessed the strength and resilience to navigate whatever challenges awaited. And this time, she wouldn't be going it alone.

As the gentle night breeze whispered through the open window, Prissy sank into the plush comfort of her bed, her body deliciously spent from the emotional exertion of her practice session. She inhaled deeply, savoring the lingering scent of the jasmine that perfumed the warm summer air.

Her mind, however, was a whirlwind of thoughts and possibilities, each one more tantalizing than the last. With a slight smile playing upon her full lips, she allowed herself to indulge in the fantasies that danced just beyond the veil of consciousness.

In her mind's eye, she envisioned Alex's chiseled features, his intense gaze boring into her with a hunger that ignited a smoldering heat low in her belly. She imagined the taut lines of his body, the corded muscles rippling beneath tanned skin as he pulled her into a searing embrace.

A soft moan escaped her parted lips as she pictured his strong hands roaming the curves of her body, his touch setting her very nerves ablaze. The mere thought of his lips trailing a scorching path along the column of her throat was enough to elicit a shiver of wanton desire.

Prissy's fingers danced across the silken sheets, her nails raking lightly over the sensitive flesh of her inner thighs as she allowed the delicious fantasy to unfold. She craved the feel of Alex's weight pinning her to the mattress, his muscular frame caging her in a delirious prison of lust and longing.

With a sharp intake of breath, she banished the tantalizing images, her cheeks flushed with a mixture of desire and shame. These were dangerous thoughts, a Pandora's box of temptation that threatened to unravel the carefully constructed tapestry of her life.

And yet, as she lay in the enveloping darkness, Prissy couldn't deny the magnetic pull she felt towards the enigmatic artist. It was a force that defied logic, a siren's call that lured her ever closer to the precipice of the unknown.

A faint smile curved her lips as she surrendered to the heady swirl of excitement and trepidation that thrummed through her veins. Tomorrow, she would confront this strange new world that beckoned, embracing the journey with equal parts determination and reckless abandon.

With a contented sigh, Prissy allowed the gentle tendrils of slumber to wrap around her, her dreams awash with the tantalizing promise of what was yet to come.

six

The incessant buzzing of her phone shattered the silence. Prissy's brow furrowed as she glanced at the caller ID - Alex Shefton. With a steadying breath, she answered, "Hello?"

"Prissy, darling," Alex's rich baritone caressed her name. "I hope I'm not calling at an inopportune time."

She tensed, suddenly aware of her shabby apartment's peeling wallpaper. "Not at all. What can I do for you?"

"I have a proposition, if you're amenable. Something that could elevate your career to stratospheric heights." His words hung heavy with implication. "But I'd prefer to discuss it in person, over a glass of the finest Château Margaux, if you're free this evening?"

Intrigue flickered within her. "What happened to 3 o'clock at the gallery?"

"Scratch that, love. I'm inviting you to my penthouse."

"Your penthouse?"

"Precisely. Shall we say, eight o'clock?"

Prissy thought about for a quick second then released, "I'll be there."

The line went dead, leaving Prissy to contemplate the evening ahead...

LATER THAT NIGHT, Prissy's modest Civic pulled up to Alex's ostentatious high-rise in Century City, with a view that overlook the ocean. She smoothed her hands over her fitted black dress, suddenly self-conscious. Taking a fortifying breath, she ascended the opulent lobby's marble steps, heels clacking against the gleaming floor.

The elevator's ascent seemed to stretch infinitely until, finally, the doors parted onto Alex's private penthouse floor. She rapped tentatively on the ornate double doors.

They swung open to reveal Alex, impeccably attired in a tailored Savile Row suit. "Prissy," he greeted warmly, eyes roving over her with unmistakable appreciation. "You look ravishing."

Heat crept up her neck. "This old thing?" She brushed aside the compliment with feigned nonchalance.

Ushering her inside, Alex's apartment exuded sophistication and wealth. Prissy drank in the elegant space - soaring ceilings, Persian rugs underfoot, walls adorned with priceless artworks.

"Welcome to my humble abode," Alex murmured, amusement flickering across his chiseled features.

"Humble?" Prissy echoed incredulously. This place could swallow her run-down apartment building whole.

His rich chuckle enveloped her like warm cognac. "A bit much, I concede. But one must have a space befitting their passions."

Those penetrating green eyes caressed her again, and Prissy flushed, suddenly overheated despite the cavernous space's pristine climate control.

Alex gestured towards an immense living room, minimalist yet sumptuous. "Make yourself comfortable. Can I offer you a drink?"

As Prissy settled onto the plush sofa, she was enveloped by the scent of fine leather and Alex's lingering cologne. "I'll have whatever you're having."

With a roguish grin, Alex procured a dusty bottle of Cristal from an antique cabinet. As he deftly popped the cork, Prissy tried not to gape at the shameless opulence surrounding her.

Two crystal flutes in hand, Alex joined her on the couch, close enough that his reassuring presence seemed to envelope her. Prissy accepted the proffered glass with a murmured thanks, their fingers brushing in a dizzying caress.

She lifted the champagne to her lips, the bubbles tickling her tongue with effervescent delight. Prissy couldn't resist a sidelong glance at her host.

Alex's gaze smoldered over the rim of his glass, twin azure flames licking at her skin. "You seem...pensive this evening," he rumbled.

Prissy wavered under that scorching scrutiny. "I - I'm just trying to wrap my head around all this." She waved a hand, indicating the palatial space. "It's a far cry from the hood."

His expression softened, eyes crinkling at the corners with understated warmth. "I forget how overwhelming this lifestyle must appear from the outside." One large hand tentatively covered hers. "But I want you to feel at home here, Prissy."

A tremor raced through her at the simple contact. *Home? In this glittering fantasyland?* Yet somehow, Alex's proximity acted as a steadying force. "I'm listening," she murmured, leaning impulsively into his solid frame.

Alex took a fortifying sip of champagne before meeting her gaze with renewed intensity. "You are an exceptional talent, Priscilla. Truly, I've never encountered an artist who can convey such raw emotion through their music." His voice thrummed with conviction. "Which is why I want – no, need – to showcase your gifts on the global stage."

Prissy's breath caught in her throat as the weight of his words sank in. *An international exhibit?* Her mind whirled, caught between dreams of grandeur and a bone-deep fear of failure.

"This is...massive." She wet her lips, torn between exhilaration and trepidation. "Alex, I'm just a girl from the projects trying to make it big. Are you sure I'm ready for that level of exposure?"

His gaze held her transfixed, stripping away every insecurity with its blazing confidence. "You were born ready, love." The endearment slipped out, underscored by the caressing timbre of his voice. "The world needs to experience the passion you pour into every note, every soulful stroke of the bow."

Prissy's pulse thundered in her ears as she contemplated the intoxicating opportunity laid before her. This was her dream, the chance to finally prove her worth on the grandest scale imaginable. Yet a litany of doubts still gnawed at her resolve. *What if she crumbled under the intense spotlight? What if her humble roots left her hopelessly outmatched among the elite talents?*

Sensing her inner turmoil, Alex reached out to tenderly brush a stray curl from her cheek. "I realize this is daunting," he murmured. "But you must believe in yourself as fervently as I believe in you, Priscilla."

His touch ignited a simmering flame within her, both thrilling and terrifying in its intensity. This man's unwavering faith in her abilities was almost overwhelming. *Could she live up to such lofty expectations?* Prissy searched the depths of those mesmerizing green eyes and found her answer.

Alex's fingers entwined with hers, sending an electric charge pulsing through her veins. "You've got this, Priscilla," he husked, the gruff timbre of his voice a stark contrast to the tender gesture.

"My girls been tellin' me to go for it," she murmured, thoughts drifting to the steadfast encouragement from her sister and closest friends. They'd been her rock, bolstering her confidence when the relentless grind threatened to crush her spirit. "Said I'd be a fool to pass up this kinda opportunity."

Despite their well-intentioned words, Alex's intense stare was more convincing. This polished and experienced man had unshakable belief in her potential to conquer the world's most prestigious stage. His trust in her abilities sparked a fierce determination within her.

"Damn, we both know I ain't about that high-society life," Prissy confessed, chewing her lip in consternation. "You really think I got what it takes to hang with them prim and proper art snobs?"

For a fleeting moment, uncertainty flickered across Alex's chiseled features. Then his expression hardened with resolve, jaw tensing beneath the shadow of his immaculately groomed stubble. "You're an artist, Priscilla. A master of your craft. That transcends any perceived class boundaries or societal constraints."

His impassioned words caressed her senses like a lover's skilled touch. This man's faith in her was unshakable, fueling an aching need to prove herself worthy of such adulation. With a steadying inhalation, Prissy steeled her nerves and squared her shoulders.

"Alright, Shefton. Let's do this thing."

Prissy's declaration seemed to siphon the air from the room, the weighted silence a visceral thing hanging between them. For a heartbeat, Alex remained motionless, his stormy gaze locked with hers in an electric trance. Then his lips curved into a devastating smile that stole her breath.

"You've no idea how profoundly your acceptance means to me," he murmured, the words laced with an undercurrent of raw emotion. Without preamble, he slid closer, the sudden proximity setting her nerves alight. "I'll be right beside you every step, Priscilla. Supporting you, believing in your immense talent."

His nearness amplified each nuanced expression, each minute shift in those green eyes now dark pools of sincerity and unveiled longing. Prissy's pulse hammered a frantic rhythm as the energy between them thickened with unspoken promises. Instinctively, she found herself leaning into his orbit, drawn by an elemental need to close the diminishing distance.

Alex's palm came to rest against her cheek in a searing caress, calloused fingers trailing heated sparks across her skin. "Let me be your muse, your tether to this wondrous world of beauty we're about to unleash upon the masses."

The timbre of his voice had deepened into a gravelly rasp that reverberated through her core. Prissy's eyelids fluttered, her senses overwhelmed by his earthy, masculine scent and the electric tingle awakening every nerve ending. This man was potent intoxication personified.

As their bodies slowly separated, her words hung in the air like a fragile spiderweb. The warmth of her breath still lingered on his skin, but he could feel the distance growing between them. "I'm counting on you to be my rock," she whispered, her voice filled with both longing and hesitation. Shefton could see the determination in her eyes as she pulled away, her hands trembling slightly. "But I understand if you don't want to blur the lines between work and pleasure."

A deep ache formed in his chest at her words, knowing that they would have to keep things strictly professional despite the undeniable chemistry between them. But he knew it was for the best, even if it meant sacrificing his own desires.

As he nodded in agreement, he couldn't help but feel a sense of unease. He stood up and tried to smooth out his wrinkled shirt and jacket, a futile attempt to hide the turmoil churning inside him. Yes, they were in agreement, but at what cost? He wasn't sure if he was ready to face the consequences of their decision.

He wanted her, this much he knew for sure. But he always wanted to showcase her talent more. Lust, could wait—for now.

He walked away from her creating distance between them. "Let's discuss our international endeavor, shall we?"

seven

The heavy oak door crashed open as Ellie barreled into her brother's office, papers askew and cheeks flushed with urgency. "Alex, I need your signature on these acquisition forms before the end of the—"

Her words trailed off as two hushed voices reached her ears from the hallway, muffled yet unmistakable in their gossipy tenor.

"That miserable cow Lottie is hosting her own bloody exhibit next month," one scathing whisper sliced through the quiet. "It'll outshine Shefton's whole production."

Ellie stilled, her brow furrowing as she strained to catch the reply. Curiosity, that ever-simmering flame, flickered to life within her breast.

"Surely she's taking the piss?" The second voice, laced with derision. "Her washed-up hacks can't hold a candle to Prissy and her... exotic talents."

A scandalized gasp and a low titter of laughter drifted in, sparking Ellie's indignation. Clutching the forms to her chest, she crept towards the doorway, her kitten heels silent on the plush carpet.

"Keep your knickers on. You know how Lottie operates - she'll stoop to any depths to stay relevant. Hell hath no fury like a desperate arthouse crone on the wane."

Ellie leaned against the doorframe, feeling the roughness of the mahogany wood against her flushed cheek. She couldn't help but listen to the conversation taking place inside, every word dripping with salacious gossip. Across the room, Alex was intently focused on paperwork at his desk, unaware of the poisonous rumors swirling around him in the shadows.

She couldn't let this slide, not with Alex's meticulous work and Prissy's breathtaking performance at stake. Teeth worrying her glossed lower lip, Ellie straightened her shoulders and marched off, papers forgotten in the wake of her burning need to uncover the truth.

Ellie's heels clacked a staccato rhythm against the polished floor as she strode through the gallery's marbled foyer, her gaze fixed on the tall, imperious figure of Charlotte "Lottie" Hargreaves up ahead. The esteemed curator's sharpened tongue and cutthroat reputation preceded her, but Ellie refused to let intimidation cloud her judgment.

Ducking behind a sleek obsidian sculpture, Ellie watched as Lottie ushered a knot of artists into a secluded alcove, their faces a blend of awe and trepidation. A sinewy hush fell over the group as Lottie's imperious tones rang out, her words a barbed lash.

"You're all competent craftsmen, I'll grant you that," she sneered, her hawkish gaze raking over the assembled talents. "But make no mistake - this is my exhibit, and you'll play by *my* rules if you want a slice of the exposure. And exposure, darlings, is the only currency that matters in our fickle little world."

Ellie's fingers tightened around the edge of the plinth, knuckles paling. Lottie's disdainful cadence grated against her ears, each sentence a fresh insult against the artistic ideals she held dear.

"That sorry sod Shefton is peddling some dancer's tawdry

floor show as high art," Lottie continued, her ruby-slashed lips curling into a serpentine smile. "Well, we'll show him the true face of sophistication. Your works will be the coup de grâce, eclipsing that insipid little harlot before she's even slipped into her first costume change."

A ripple of uneasy laughter broke the tension, but Ellie felt her hackles rise at the brazen disrespect leveled at Prissy's talents. She leaned in closer, determined to unearth every last damning detail of Lottie's underhanded scheme.

Ellie's narrowed gaze bored into the curator's hawkish profile as Lottie outlined her grand vision, each grandiose boast a twist of the dagger in her brother's back. But the final proclamation seared itself into Ellie's consciousness, galvanizing her resolve.

"When this is over, Shefton will be a laughingstock - a has-been curator trading on faded glories while the rest of us bask in the limelight. Mark my words..."

Ellie had heard enough. Turning on her heel, she scanned the milling artists until her gaze settled on a young woman standing apart from the others. Her posture was guarded, arms crossed defensively as she listened to Lottie's tirade with a conflicted expression.

This was her chance.

Adjusting her silk scarf, Ellie plastered a polite smile on her face and approached the solitary figure. "Pardon me," she began, her cultured tones cutting through the din. "I couldn't help but notice you seem...ambivalent about this whole affair."

The woman started, hazel eyes widening briefly before narrowing in suspicion. "Who are you? One of Lottie's lackeys?"

"Heavens, no." Ellie forced a tinkling laugh, willing the other woman to relax. "I'm merely an interested observer, that's all. But I must admit, I'm a tad...concerned by some of the things I've overheard."

Her companion's shoulders tensed, but there was a glimmer of curiosity in her eyes now. "Such as?"

Bingo. Ellie leaned closer, pitching her voice low. "Well, it seems our esteemed curator has rather...unsavory intentions. Using people's art as mere pawns in some power play against another gallery? Tsk tsk, it's dreadfully uncouth."

The other woman shifted uncomfortably, chewing her lower lip. "I...I had my suspicions, but..."

"But you need this exhibition, don't you?" Ellie murmured sympathetically. "A harsh reality we artists must all face at times."

A curt nod was her only answer, but it was enough. Sensing an opening, Ellie pressed on. "I don't mean to pry, but...if you had an alternative? A chance to have your work appreciated on its own merits, without being wielded as ammunition in someone else's petty vendetta?"

The woman's eyes narrowed again, but there was yearning there, too. A desperate hunger for recognition that resonated deeply with Ellie. "I'm listening..."

Leaning fractionally closer, Ellie allowed a conspirator's smile to ghost across her lips. "Perhaps we can be of mutual benefit to one another..."

ELLIE HURRIED BACK to Alex's office, her mind whirling with the revelations she'd uncovered. Lottie was even more underhanded than she'd imagined—using up-and-coming artists as mere pawns in her twisted game against Alex. The thought made Ellie's blood boil.

She swept into the sleek, modern space, tossing her handbag onto the plush sofa with a huff. Striding over to the floor-to-ceiling windows, she stared out at the downtown Los Angeles skyline, the city's iconic landmarks casting long shadows in the fading evening light.

"That manipulative cow," Ellie muttered, hands on her hips. *How dare Lottie try to sabotage Alex's big break like this? After all his years of hard work and sacrifice, clawing his way up from humble beginnings.* He deserved his success, not to have it snatched away by that...that harpy's machinations.

Pivoting on her heel, Ellie began to pace the posh office space, her kitten heels clicking sharply on the hardwood floors. She had to fight fire with fire. Protect Alex's reputation and his show at all costs—by any means necessary.

First step: research. Ellie made a beeline for Alex's massive oak desk, booting up his computer. Her fingers flew over the keyboard as she dove into Lottie's past exhibits, sponsorships, professional connections. Looking for weaknesses to exploit, any chink in that polished armor.

Hours ticked by as she pored over files, scribbling frantic notes until her hand cramped. Lottie was ruthlessly effective, she'd give her that. But everyone had skeletons, dark secrets buried deep. Ellie just had to unearth them.

Idea after idea began percolating as her research progressed. Suddenly, she straightened, eyes alight with determination. *Of course—fight flash with flash!* If Lottie wanted to put on a gaudy, overblown spectacle, they'd match it and then some.

Reaching for her mobile, Ellie began making calls, her posh accent taking on a brisk, businesslike cadence. Critics, bloggers, social media influencers—she rallied them all for Prissy's big night. Lining up glowing reviews, drumming up buzz, stoking public frenzy.

This wasn't just about Alex's show anymore. It was about cementing Prissy as the true star, the one luminous talent that would outshine all others. No cheap parlor tricks, just raw, bleeding talent to transfix the masses.

By night's end, an intricate web of media hype was already taking shape. *Just a taste of what was to come,* Ellie vowed, the first salvo in her counteroffensive against Lottie's insidious ploys.

Weary but galvanized, she sank into the plush leather chair behind Alex's desk. Her gaze drifted to the framed family photos scattered across its surface—her parents beaming with pride, Alex resplendent in his graduation robes.

"Don't worry, poppet," Ellie murmured, gently tracing her fingertip over the image. "Big sis has got your back. That petty bitch hasn't a clue what's coming for her."

The relish in her voice was unmistakable as the first slivers of her master strategy took shape. She would protect Alex's legacy and humble Lottie in one fell swoop.

She had to speak to Priscilla Alexander ... and fast.

THE HEAVY OAK door swung open, and Alex strode into the room, his jaw clenched and eyes narrowed. He raked them over the two women, equal parts perplexed and annoyed by their little soiree.

"Would someone mind illuminating me as to what's so bloody important that it couldn't wait?" His cultured tones dripped with thinly veiled impatience.

Ellie straightened in her chair, her chin tilting upwards defiantly. "It's Lottie, that duplicitous worm. She means to undermine your exhibit with one of her own."

Alex's scowl deepened as he lowered himself into the buttery leather chair behind his desk. "Preposterous. That has-been couldn't curate her way out of a paper sack."

"Don't be so smug, Alex," Prissy chimed in, swirling the dregs of her rapidly cooling drink. "Your little sis did some digging, and this chick is straight up ruthless. She's got bank and some big name artists already on board. Should I be worried?"

Running a hand through his meticulously groomed hair, Alex studied them shrewdly. "No, love—let's have it then. What brilliant stratagem have you two dreamt up?"

Ellie cleared her throat and rattled off their proposed tactics —a full-court media blitz, high-profile collaborators to bolster

Prissy's gravitas, pop-up exhibits to whet the public's appetite. Her speech was measured but laced with urgency.

"We must be relentless in ensuring Prissy outshines that harpy at every turn," she concluded. "No stone unturned, no slight overlooked until she slinks back to whatever rat hole she crawled out of."

Reclining in his chair, Alex pursed his lips as a pensive silence stretched between them. Finally, he sat forward, bracing his hands on the desk as he appraised them evenly.

"You make a compelling case," he admitted, features smoothing into a wry smile. "Though I do so hate being out-maneuvered, especially by that miserable old trout. Very well, you have my support. Do whatever is required to preserve my—*our*—reputation. Lord knows we can't have the riffraff thinking they've one over on us."

Prissy rolled her eyes but said nothing, merely knocking back the last dregs of her now tepid drink. This stuffy display of nobility and self-importance never failed to rankle her sensibilities.

Ellie, however, looked triumphant. A feral glint flickered in her eyes as she stood, back ramrod straight.

"Excellent. Then we haven't a moment to waste. Let the games begin."

OVER THE NEXT FEW DAYS, a palpable energy coursed through Alex's opulent office suite. Ellie was a whirlwind of activity, juggling a dizzying array of tasks with her usual unflappable efficiency.

She fired off rapid-fire emails, her fingers flying across the keyboard as she coordinated interviews and publicity opportunities. With Prissy's input, she carefully curated a lineup of guest performers—bold voices from various artistic disciplines—to share the stage and amplify the cellist's magnetism.

"We want them eatin' outta the palm of my hand," Prissy declared in one of their strategy sessions. "This shindig's gotta sizzle so hot, Lottie gets burned just thinking about it."

Ellie smirked at the bravado, making a note on her ever-present tablet. "Consider it done. When we're through, the entire art world will be buzzing about you, gorgeous."

Meanwhile, Alex played to his strengths, leveraging his extensive connections to garner endorsements from heavyweight critics and tastemakers. His silver tongue and cultured charm proved invaluable, ensuring a cavalcade of radiant reviews awaited Prissy's debut.

"One gets what one works for," he told Prissy with an indulgent smile. "Though I dare say your raw talent smoothed the way. They'll be eating out of your delightfully calloused hands, poppet."

As the big night drew near, a current of nervous exhilaration thrummed through the trio. Ellie's strategic bombshells were primed, Prissy's performance had been finely honed to perfection, and Alex's web of influential admirers stood at the ready.

On the eve of the exhibition's grand opening, they convened in Alex's study over tumblers of well-aged scotch. Ellie's eyes danced with fiery determination as she raised her glass.

"To weathering any storm," she toasted with a decisive nod. "We face Lottie's pathetic gambit united, strong, and assured of our triumph. She hasn't a prayer against our combined brilliance."

Prissy and Alex echoed the toast, clinking their glasses together in a ritual of unflinching resolve. No upstart, no matter how ruthless, could impede their ambition.

eight

The smoky haze of the jazz club enveloped Prissy as she sat across from Rafe in their corner nook, the sultry notes of the saxophonist drifting over them like a lover's caress. Her cello rested against the table, and Rafe's guitar leaned casually beside him - their constant companions in this dimly lit sanctum.

Rafe leaned forward, his brow furrowed with concern as he studied her face. "You know this international exhibit could be your big break, chica," he said, his voice low and husky. "But I can't help worryin' what it might mean for us."

Prissy's gaze met his, her dark eyes shimmering with a kaleidoscope of emotions. "Rafe, you know I've been workin' towards this my whole life," she murmured, her full lips curving into a slight frown. "Don't you want me to spread my wings?"

He let out a frustrated sigh, running a hand through his tousled hair. "Course I do, querida. But this place..." He gestured towards the stage where their fellow musicians swayed and crooned. "It's our home, our family. I don't wanna lose what we've built together."

Prissy's chest tightened as she regarded the man before her -

her closest friend, her musical soulmate. She understood his fears all too well, the prospect of change sending tremors through her own heart. But the siren call of ambition, the yearning for something more, drowned out her trepidation.

"Rafe," she said softly, her voice laced with determination. "You know this opportunity could open doors for me I've only dreamed of. But you're right - this place, our music, it's everything to me too."

Prissy reached across the table, her slender fingers wrapping around Rafe's calloused hand. "Listen to me, baby," she said, her voice a gentle cadence amidst the jazzy melodies surrounding them. "No matter where this path takes me, you and me, we're tied together tighter than a sailor's knot."

Rafe's thumb traced slow circles against her skin, his dark eyes searching hers. "You say that now, but how can you be so sure, huh?" he challenged, a hint of desperation creeping into his tone. "This big, fancy exhibit could sweep you off to places I can't follow."

Prissy held his gaze, her expression a portrait of unwavering conviction. "Rafe, you're more than just my partner on that stage," she said, nodding towards the performers bathed in pale spotlights. "You're my brother, my family. Distance ain't never gonna change that."

A heavy silence settled between them, punctuated only by the sultry notes of a saxophone solo. Rafe's features softened, his shoulders sagging slightly as the tension seeped from his muscles. "Alright, chica," he relented with a weary sigh. "I trust you. Just promise me one thing?"

Prissy quirked an eyebrow, her plush lips curving into a faint smile. "What's that?"

Rafe leaned forward, his gaze smoldering with a fiery intensity. "Promise you won't forget about this broke-ass guitar player when you're a big star on the international scene."

"Forget about you?" she murmured, her voice a husky whisper. "That ain't never gonna happen, Rafe."

Vulnerability flickered across her features as she allowed the weight of her fears to surface. "Truth is, I'm terrified of leaving all this behind. This place, these people..." She gestured vaguely around the dimly lit club, her gaze lingering on the familiar faces that had become her extended family. "It's like a damn security blanket, you feel me?"

Rafe's thumb traced the curve of her cheekbone, his touch a gentle anchor amidst the turbulence of her emotions. "I feel you, mami," he assured her, his rich baritone laced with empathy. "But you gotta let go of that blanket sometimes, spread those wings and fly."

A wistful smile tugged at the corners of Prissy's mouth. "When did you get so damn wise, Rafe Martinez?"

He flashed her a rakish grin, the familiar spark of mischief dancing in his eyes. "I've always been a genius, baby. You just been too busy making sweet, sweet music to notice."

Prissy rolled her eyes, but her laughter mingled with the soulful notes that filled the air, a harmonious blend that spoke of the unbreakable bond they shared. In that moment, she knew – no matter where her journey took her, Rafe would always be a part of her melody, a constant refrain in the symphony of her life.

Prissy's gaze met Rafe's, her eyes shimmering with a depth of emotion that words could scarcely capture. "You know you mean more to me than just about anyone in this world, right?" she murmured, her voice thick with sentiment.

Rafe's calloused fingers intertwined with hers, the calluses a testament to the countless hours they had devoted to their craft. "And you're my heart, mami," he replied, his usual bravado tempered by raw sincerity. "This connection we have, it's deeper than the music. It's like our souls are intertwined, dancing to a rhythm only we can hear."

A shuddering breath escaped Prissy's lips as she fought against the swell of feelings that threatened to overwhelm her. She had always prided herself on her independence, her ability to forge her own path without needing to rely on anyone else. But Rafe had a way of stripping away her defenses, leaving her bare and vulnerable in a way that both terrified and exhilarated her.

"I don't know what I'd do without you, Rafe," she confessed, her fingers tightening around his as if to anchor herself to him. "You've been my rock, my partner in crime, my..." She trailed off, the words failing her as she struggled to encapsulate the enormity of what he meant to her.

Rafe leaned closer, his forehead nearly touching hers, his eyes smoldering with an intensity that sent a shiver down her spine. "I ain't going nowhere, Priss," he vowed, his tone low and gravelly. "No matter where this crazy ride takes us, you and me? We're gonna be making beautiful music together till the very end."

In that moment, the world around them faded away, the thrum of the music and the chatter of the crowd receding into a distant hum. All that existed was the two of them, bound by a connection that transcended mere friendship or artistic collaboration. It was a bond forged in the fires of shared passion, tempered by adversity, and strengthened by an unshakable trust that knew no bounds.

In all honesty, her very first performance was thanks to Rafe's smooth-talking abilities. He convinced the owner of Mo's to take a chance on her and add her cello playing to their already thriving trio. It was a risk, but they managed to make it work seamlessly. Together, their quartet became the talk of the town, drawing in crowds night after night with their daring, innovative sound. As each year passed, their music only grew more daring and original, and soon the once modest jazz club was overflowing with enthusiastic patrons every single night. The air buzzed with excitement and anticipation as people poured into the club, eager to witness the magic created by this talented quartet.

As their foreheads touched, Prissy felt a sense of peace wash over her, a certainty that no matter what challenges lay ahead, she would never be alone. With Rafe by her side, she could conquer the world.

Rafe leaned back in his chair, a mischievous glint in his eyes as he surveyed the dimly lit jazz club, the smoky air thick with the scent of whiskey and desire. His gaze settled on Prissy, drinking in the sight of her—the delicate curve of her jaw, the way her lips curled into a subtle smile, the loose tendrils of hair that framed her face like a crown of midnight silk.

"You know," he said, his voice a low rumble that sent a delicious shiver down her spine, "if you're really gonna leave this place behind, we gotta make sure we leave our mark." He reached across the table, his calloused fingers grazing the back of her hand, a gesture that felt like a brand against her skin. "Let's make some memories that'll have 'em talkin' for years to come, Priss."

Prissy arched an eyebrow, her lips twitching with barely contained amusement. "You got something in mind, hot shot?"

Rafe flashed her a wolfish grin, his eyes dancing with unspoken promises. "Oh, I got plenty in mind, baby girl. Trust me, by the time we're done, this place ain't never gonna be the same."

A burst of raucous laughter escaped Prissy's lips, a sound so pure and unfettered that it seemed to cut through the haze of smoke and tension that hung in the air. It was a moment of pure, unadulterated joy, a glimpse of the carefree spirit that lurked beneath her carefully cultivated facade.

"Alright, Rafe," she conceded, her eyes sparkling with mischief. "Let's show 'em what we're made of."

And just like that, their worries melted away, replaced by a shared sense of exhilaration and anticipation. For tonight, at least, they were masters of their own destiny, two kindred spirits united in their love for the music that coursed through their veins like lifeblood.

As the band struck up a soulful melody, Prissy and Rafe exchanged a knowing glance, a silent promise passing between them.

Tonight, they would create magic.

nine

With a soft creak, the door swung open, revealing the stunning figure of Prissy Alexander. She radiated grace and passion, her mere presence causing Alex to catch his breath in awe. It had been weeks since he had last seen her, and now as she stood before him, he was filled with excitement to begin their collaboration. He had chosen her to be the musical centerpiece for high-scale art exhibits in prestigious cities like Beverly Hills, Boston, and New York, and he knew she would elevate each event to new heights with her talent and charm.

Her warm smile stretched across full lips, her eyes sparkling with excitement.

"Come on in, Alex." Prissy stepped aside, welcoming him into her domain.

Alex nodded, his heart pounding in his chest. "Thank you, Prissy. I'm looking forward to our session."

He followed her into the living room, his gaze trailing over the plush furnishings and the cello case propped open, sheet music scattered nearby. A true artist's den.

"Make yourself comfy." Prissy gestured toward the couch, her fingers trailing along the cello's smooth surface as she retrieved it from the case. "I'll be right with you."

Alex sank into the cushions, his eyes fixated on Prissy's slender form as she cradled the instrument. With practiced ease, she settled into the chair, the cello nestled between her thighs like a cherished lover.

Prissy quirked a brow, her full lips curving into a sultry smirk. "I've been working a few familiar sets—and something new—are you ready for this?"

Alex swallowed hard, his throat suddenly dry. "Absolutely, darling. Let's make some magic."

Prissy's fingers danced across the strings, coaxing out a few warm-up notes. The rich, resonant tones filled the air, caressing Alex's senses. He closed his eyes, allowing the music to wash over him, stirring desires he thought long buried.

This woman was pure temptation, and Alex found himself helpless to resist her siren call.

Prissy's fingers continued to glide across the strings, the warm-up notes giving way to a hauntingly beautiful melody. Alex watched, transfixed, as her body swayed with the music, lost in the moment.

Her brow furrowed in concentration, those full lips parted ever so slightly. Alex found himself mesmerized by the play of emotions across her features – passion, vulnerability, raw sensuality. It was as if Prissy poured her very soul into each note, weaving a tapestry of sound that ensnared his senses.

He shifted in his seat, uncomfortably aware of the growing ache in his loins. Prissy's performance was pure seduction, an intimate dance that left him aching for her touch, her taste, her warmth.

"Breathtaking," he murmured, his voice husky with want.

Prissy's lashes fluttered open, her dark eyes locking with his. A slow, knowing smile curved those luscious lips. "You like what you see?"

"More than you could possibly imagine," Alex confessed, his cultured veneer slipping.

She hummed in approval, never faltering in her playing. "Then sit back and enjoy the show."

As the sultry strains filled the air, Alex knew he was helplessly ensnared in Prissy's web. This fierce, talented vixen had claimed him, body and soul, with nothing more than her music.

And he wouldn't have it any other way.

Prissy's cello solo built to a trembling crescendo, the notes seeming to vibrate through Alex's very core. He found himself utterly spellbound, drawn into the vortex of her artistry.

As the intensity ebbed, Alex cleared his throat. "Exquisite, as always. Though I wonder..." He rose fluidly and approached her music stand. "If you adjusted your bowing technique like this..."

Gently, he placed his hand over hers, guiding the movement of the bow across the strings. Prissy stiffened at his touch, her nostrils flaring. For a beat, Alex thought she might rebuff him. Then her shoulders relaxed, allowing his guidance.

"I see what you mean," she murmured, her honeyed voice sliding over him. "Let me try it..."

Obediently, she mirrored the subtle shift in technique. The notes took on a richer, more resonant quality, vibrating through the air between them. Alex hummed deep in his throat, adding his voice in soaring counterpoint.

Too soon, the spell was broken. They drew apart, chests heaving, pulses pounding. Prissy's gaze smoldered over him, equal parts challenge and invitation.

"Damn, Mr. Shelton," she purred. "Didn't know you could spit bars like that."

A lazy smirk tugged at his lips. "There's a great deal you have yet to discover about me, Miss Alexander."

Her tongue traced her full lower lip. "Oh, I plan to explore every delicious secret you're hiding..."

The erotic promise in her words sent desire searing through

him. Alex's fingers clenched with the need to yank her against him, to lose himself in her lush curves.

This woman wasn't just getting under his skin – she was burrowing straight into his soul.

Despite the thrumming tension, Alex forced himself to focus on the task at hand. "Speaking of secrets, what piece did you have in mind for the exhibit?"

Prissy's expression sobered as she considered. "I want something raw, you know? Like, gut-punching and stripped bare." She idly plucked at the cello strings. "Most folks expect pretty, polished perfection. But real art? It grabs you by the throat and don't let go."

Alex nodded slowly. She was absolutely right – the greatest works laid the creator's spirit naked before the world. "A bold choice. I take it you have something specific in mind?"

"Maybe *Shostakovich's Cello Concerto No. 1*?" She chewed her lip. "It's a beast, technically. But the emotion in it..." She trailed off with a shudder.

His breath caught. That particular concerto was a shattering lament of anguish and defiance under Soviet oppression. For Prissy to convey its depths would require exposing the rawest, darkest corners of her soul to the audience.

"An ambitious selection," he murmured. "Are you certain you wish to take on such a...revealing work?"

Her gaze locked with his, unflinching. "I don't do this for applause or accolades, Alex. I play because the music owns me, body and soul. If I'm gonna bare it all, I might as well go all the way, right?"

The raw hunger in her tone sent a shiver down his spine. This woman was embracing the very heart of what it meant to be an artist – the vulnerability, the sacrifice, the metamorphosis of pain into transcendent beauty.

He gave a solemn nod of respect. "Then we shall ensure your performance does justice to that searing truth."

Alex leaned back, digesting the weight of Prissy's vision. "I couldn't agree more about striving for raw, unvarnished truth in performance. Though perhaps we could enhance the sensory experience further..."

He clasped his hands, eyes alight with inspiration. "What if we incorporated visual elements? Projections or dynamic lighting to underscore the emotional beats? If curated with care, the right imagery could lend powerful subtext, juxtaposing light and shadow, hope and despair."

Prissy cocked her head, intrigued. "You talkin' like, a whole multimedia thing? That could be dope as hell if we do it right." Her fingers danced in the air as she envisioned the possibilities. "Maybe some grainy, black-and-white footage of Soviet workers, all grim faces and empty bellies. Then wham – hit 'em with splashes of vivid color during the hopeful crescendos."

"Precisely," Alex purred in approval. "Striking visuals to heighten the emotional resonance. Guide the audience's hearts and minds in visceral lockstep with the music's narrative arc."

He reached for a notepad, scribbling concepts as they riffed back and forth, sparks flying. Prissy stood, cello abandoned as she prowled the room, acting out staging ideas with theatrical flair.

"OK-alright, I'm feelin' this..." She paused mid-stride, smirking mischievously at him over one shoulder. "But I need a break first. Whatch'u think about some tea, fancy Brit?"

Alex blinked, momentarily thrown. "You...drink tea?"

A rich, smoky chuckle rolled from her lips. "What, you thought 'cause I'm a sista, I only drink 40s and purple drank?"

"Not at all!" He raised his hands defensively, a sheepish grin tugging his mouth. "I simply didn't take you for a tea enthusiast."

Prissy winked, hips swaying as she slipped into the kitchen. "Hope you like it sweet as sin."

Alex chuckled under his breath, slouching on the couch. This woman was endlessly surprising, sensual and audacious one moment, warmly disarming the next. He found the whiplash between her contrasting facets utterly captivating.

Prissy soon returned, carefully balancing two steaming mugs of fragrant tea. Handing one to Alex, she nestled into the couch beside him, knees pulled up and body angled to face him.

"Thanks, love," he murmured, inhaling the rich aroma with an appreciative smirk. He took a tentative sip, eyebrows shooting up. "Good Lord, how much sugar did you put in here?"

"Just how I like it," she shrugged, grinning impishly over the rim of her own mug. "Sweet 'nough to rot them fancy European teeth."

Prissy's playful ribbing struck an unexpected nerve, her barb about his privileged upbringing hitting closer to home than she knew. Alex's smile faltered for just a moment before he recovered with a soft chuckle.

"I'll have you know these are entirely American choppers, you cheeky minx."

They shared an easy laugh, but Prissy didn't miss the split-second shift in his expression, that fleeting hint of...what? Darkness? Pain? An enigmatic melancholy she sensed he kept carefully buried.

The weight of expectations, both self-imposed and external, suddenly felt heavier on her shoulders. Prissy worried her bottom lip, considering whether to confide her gnawing fears about the upcoming performance.

"Alex..." She hesitated, fingers tracing the mug's curved handle. "Can I be real with you for a sec?"

His gaze sharpened, instantly attentive to her somber tone. "Of course, Prissy. You can share anything with me."

Drawing a steadying breath, she said, "I'm low-key terrified I'm gonna choke under the pressure. This exhibit is huge for my career, you know? All them rich, snobby art folks expecting some deep-moving masterpiece from the inner city Black girl with the cello." Prissy shook her head, mouth twisting wryly.

"What if I bomb? If I can't deliver and let everybody down, I..."

"Priscilla." Alex cut her off firmly, setting his tea aside to grasp her hand. His grip was warm, calloused fingers gently squeezing her knuckles. "You are one of the most astoundingly talented musicians I've ever witnessed. Your passion, your authenticity...it's bloody extraordinary."

His piercing gaze held her transfixed as he spoke with quiet intensity. "You were born to stunning ovations, not failures. I believe in you utterly...and so should you."

A shuddering exhalation escaped Prissy's lips, equal parts disbelief and relief. Alex's steadfast belief in her abilities was almost overwhelming. She suddenly felt absurdly close to tears.

Swallowing hard, she squeezed his hand fiercely. "Thanks, Alex ... I really needed to hear that, for real."

Before Prissy could second-guess herself, she leaned forward and enveloped him in a fierce embrace. Alex froze for only an instant before wrapping his arms tightly around her, holding her slim frame flush against his chest.

They clung together, eyes squeezed shut, drawing strength and solace from the other's solid presence. When Prissy finally pulled back, there were indeed glistening tears clinging to her thick lashes.

Alex reached up, tenderly brushing them away with his thumb. Their faces hovered perilously close, heated breaths mingling. The air felt thick, charged with tension and the electric promise of more.

Just then, Alex abruptly disentangled himself, twisting away to snatch something from his satchel.

"I, ah...I have something for you." He cleared his throat awkwardly, movements suddenly jerky and self-conscious.

When he turned back, he was holding a sleek, leather-bound journal, embossed with her initials in gilded calligraphy. Prissy gasped, hands flying to her mouth.

"Oh Alex...this is gorgeous," she murmured in awe, gingerly accepting the beautiful gift. "You shouldn't have."

He shrugged, cheeks flushed, the cocky mask slipping back into place. "Well, a virtuoso needs somewhere inspiration to keep all her brilliant ideas, doesn't she?"

Prissy gazed up at him through her lashes, profoundly touched by his thoughtfulness. And just like that, the intimate tension crackled to life once more, hanging heavily between them like a living thing.

Prissy's grip tightened almost imperceptibly on the journal as she held Alex's gaze. Her pulse thrummed with an exhilarating mix of nerves and undeniable want. She drew a fortifying breath.

"We should...probably call it a day, yeah?" she ventured, flashing a rueful smile. As much as she craved Alex's nearness, they were both too emotionally wrung out to be fully present.

Alex seemed to read her mind, giving a curt nod of agreement. "Quite. We've made excellent progress, but there's still more work to be done."

Prissy tried not to dwell on the tinge of regret coloring his tone. She stretched languidly, her lithe form unfurling like a cat after a nap. "Yes, I guess I'll see you out then."

They moved towards the entryway in loaded silence, shoulders occasionally brushing in the close quarters. Prissy's mind raced - *should she just let him go?* The thought made her chest seize up. *She had to know...*

Resting one hand on the doorknob, she spun to face him, chin lifted in determination. "Alex...would you maybe wanna grab dinner sometime? Ya know, discuss things further in a more relaxed setting?"

His piercing green eyes widened briefly in surprise before crinkling at the corners, lips curving upwards. "I'd be delighted. Shall we say...this Friday evening?"

Relief and excitement bloomed in Prissy's chest. "Sounds

perfect." She matched his smile with one of her own, bright and dimpled.

Alex reached out, tucking an escaped curl behind her ear with maddening tenderness. "Until then, my dear."

Prissy shivered at his husky murmur and the intimate endearment. As he brushed past into the hallway, their bodies skimmed tantalizingly close. She inhaled the lingering traces of his cologne - sandalwood and citrus with a darker, muskier undertone. Intoxicating.

With a roguish wink, Alex disappeared around the corner, leaving Prissy flushed and reeling in his wake. She slumped back against the door, clutching the journal to her thundering heart.

No matter what happened, one thing was certain - that Friday night couldn't come soon enough.

Prissy barely slept that night, tossing and turning as thoughts of Alex consumed her mind. His refined British accent, those intense green eyes, the way his touch had set her skin tingling...

FRIDAY EVENING FINALLY ARRIVED, and Prissy fussed over her appearance like a nervous teenager before a first date. *Should she wear the slinky black dress that hugged her curves? Or the flowy red number that made her look more sophisticated?*

In the end, she settled on a deep green wrap dress that brought out the warm tones in her complexion. With a few deft touches of makeup and a spritz of her favorite jasmine perfume, she stepped back to admire her reflection. "Girl, you got this," she murmured, smoothing her hands over the silky fabric.

The knock at the door made her heart leap into her throat. She drew a steadying breath before pulling it open to reveal Alex, looking impeccably handsome as always in a charcoal gray suit. He held out a bottle of rich red wine with a roguish grin.

"For you, my dear. Shall we?"

Prissy accepted the bottle with a dazzling smile, unable to tear her eyes away from the smoldering heat in his gaze. "We shall."

As she locked up her apartment, Prissy's pulse raced with a thrilling mixture of desire and trepidation. *Where would this evening lead?* Part of her was terrified to find out...but a much larger part couldn't wait to discover Alex's secrets.

The tension crackled between them like a live wire as they headed to his car. Prissy's steps faltered for a moment when he opened the passenger door of his sleek black Jaguar, every inch the sophisticated gentleman. She shot him a wry grin as she slid inside. "Fancy ride for a Brit."

Alex chuckled richly as he circled around to the driver's side. "One of my few indulgences, I must confess."

The huskiness in his tone made heat bloom low in Prissy's belly as the engine purred to life. This man would surely be the death of her...but what a way to go.

As they merged into traffic, Prissy stole sidelong glances at the chiseled profile of her companion. His earlier vulnerability had faded, replaced by an aura of unshakable confidence and control. Just who was the real Alex Shefton?

Prissy couldn't wait to find out. Her fingertips tingled with the urge to reach across the console and brush against his thigh, to see if she could ruffle that immaculate exterior...

ten

Prissy traced the perimeter of her sparsely decorated apartment, each step a measured beat in an impromptu rhythm only she could hear. Her slender fingers entwined and untwined as if wringing the last remnants of doubt from their tips, a silent sonata of worry playing through her mind. Alex Shefton—his name alone curled within her thoughts like smoke, insistent and impossible to clear. The connection between them was undeniable, a magnetic pull that tugged at the edges of her fiercely guarded heart.

The night out together was a tantalizing, teasing prelude to what she knew would eventually come between them. Every moment of the evening, her mind was consumed with thoughts of him exploring her body, his touch igniting sparks of desire within her. She had vowed to keep their relationship strictly professional, but the magnetic pull between them was impossible to deny or resist. As they laughed and talked over dinner, she couldn't help but feel the electricity crackling between them. Though they tried to keep things platonic, the intensity of their chemistry was almost suffocating, making it hard to push aside their mutual attraction.

As the night sky darkened and their dinner came to an end, he surprised her by not leaning in for a kiss or even batting an eyelash in her direction. Instead, he kept their conversation strictly professional and detached. Her frustration simmered like a pot on low heat, filling her with an inexplicable longing for something more from him. She hated this restrained version of him, longing for the playful and flirty man she knew lurked just beneath the surface.

Prissy paused by the window, clutching the sill as if it were the neck of her cello, grounding her. Outside, the city hummed with indifference to her turmoil.

"Girl, what you doin'?" she chided herself under her breath, employing the same urban American slang that connected her to her roots. She cast a glance at the collection of framed accolades adorning the walls—testaments to her disciplined solitude. Each certificate and review was a fortress she had built around herself, brick by painstaking brick.

"Feelings don't play fair," she murmured, the words barely escaping her lips before the sharp trill of the doorbell sliced through the air, slicing through her reverie like the bow on strings during a fortissimo passage.

Her heart hiccupped, then raced—a staccato rhythm that betrayed her composure. The doorbell's insistence was a harbinger of change, a pivotal note in the composition of her life that awaited resolution. Prissy hesitated, her hand hovering over the doorknob as if it were Pandora's box, containing equal parts hope and potential devastation.

"Get it together, Prissy," she whispered, her voice laced with the kind of self-reproof one might use when standing at the edge of a precipice, both drawn to the abyss and repelled by it.

With a resolve that surprised even herself, Prissy propelled her body toward the door, allowing the inertia of her decision to carry her forward. She smoothed a hand over her hair, cursing the curls that refused to be tamed, much like the emotions she struggled to corral.

She exhaled a breath, trying to steady the frantic beat of her heart, and opened the door. Her pulse hammered against her ribs, a primal drumbeat heralding the arrival of the unknown, the door swinging wide to reveal what—or who—destiny had conspired to place upon her threshold.

Prissy's gaze alighted upon the figure before her. Alex stood on the threshold, dressed in casual attire: black jeans, white shirt with a cream jacket. His smile effused warmth, the corners of his eyes crinkling in genuine delight—a testament to the mirth that seemed to light him from within whenever he beheld her.

"Evening, Priscilla," he greeted, his voice a smooth baritone that held the faintest trace of an accent polished by years away from his homeland.

"Alex," she replied, her voice a whisper, betraying the tumultuous sea of emotions roiling beneath her collected exterior. His presence was like a beacon, slicing through the fog of her apprehension, and for a fleeting moment, the world beyond the confines of her apartment ceased to exist.

Before she could regain her equilibrium or conjure up the walls she had meticulously built around her heart, Alex stepped aside to display a large box, wrapped in paper that shimmered like moonlight on a tranquil lake. It was bound with a velvet ribbon, the color of midnight, a stark contrast to the ethereal wrapping.

"For you," he said, a conspiratorial gleam playing in his eye, as if they were accomplices in a secret only they were privy to.

"Is that so?" Prissy couldn't help the note of skepticism that threaded through her words. She took the offering, her fingers grazing his—sending a jolt of electricity that she felt to the marrow of her bones. His touch was an unwelcome reminder of the danger he posed to her carefully constructed defenses.

As she peeled back the layers of paper, her hands trembled,

betraying her outward poise. The façade of nonchalance she had spent years perfecting now lay in shambles at her feet, and she cursed inwardly for allowing this man—the embodiment of everything she had convinced herself she could do without—to see her so undone.

The final fold of paper fell away, and there it lay in its case—a cello of such exquisite craftsmanship that Prissy's breath hitched in her throat. The wood glowed with a warm, honeyed patina, the grains flowing like liquid bronze, rich and deep. It was the kind of instrument that didn't just sing; it whispered secrets and dreams into the eager air. She traced a finger along the purfling, marveling at the delicate inlay work, each curl and whorl a testament to an artisan's love affair with creation.

"Alex..." she began, her voice a mere shadow amidst the awe that filled the room. "This... this is too much."

He watched her, his smile tinged with something akin to reverence. "It reminded me of you," he said softly, stepping closer. "Elegant, unique, with a depth of emotion that speaks without words. When I saw it, I could hear you playing, and the world faded into silence. This cello... it deserves a musician who can give it life, as you do with every note you coax from the strings."

Prissy felt the sting of tears threatening to spill over. His words were more than a compliment; they were an intimate acknowledgment of her soul's yearnings articulated through music. *How had he seen through the armor she wore so religiously?* Her gratitude mingled with a wild surge of vulnerability, emotions raw and searching.

"Thank you, Alex," she managed, her voice threaded with a tremulous sincerity that made her inwardly cringe. "No one has ever... believed in my music like you do." She blinked rapidly, willing the tears not to fall. To cry now would be to admit that his gesture had reached a place in her heart she hadn't realized was parched for recognition.

He stepped forward, placing a hand on her shoulder,

grounding her in the present. "Belief," he said with a quiet intensity, "is merely recognizing the truth that already exists. And Prissy, your talent is the most irrefutable truth I've encountered."

Their eyes met, and in his gaze, she found a mirror reflecting back her own fears and desires—intertwined and inseparable. For a moment, the world wasn't composed of the dichotomies she clung to: black and white, strength and vulnerability, solitude and connection. There was only the shared space between them, charged with the promise of notes yet unplayed.

Prissy's slender fingers traced the curve of the cello's neck, her touch reverent as she lifted it from its velvet-lined case. The instrument was substantial, its weight a comforting solidity against her hip, grounding her in the tangible world while her mind soared into realms of possibility. She felt the smoothness of the wood, the grain visible beneath the rich varnish like rivers of chocolate against mahogany—a tactile map of musical potential.

"May I?" she asked, her voice low and husky with a concoction of emotions too potent to name.

"Of course," Alex replied, stepping back to give her space.

She positioned the cello between her knees, the coolness of the endpin a sharp contrast to the warmth of the wood against her skin. As she tightened the bow, Prissy could feel the strings' resistance beneath her fingertips, a silent promise of the melodies they would yield to her coaxing.

"Sometimes, I think maybe I'm foolin' myself, thinking music can be my whole world. But then someone like you comes along, and it feels like maybe I ain't so crazy after all." Her laugh was a nervous flutter, betraying the tightrope walk of her composure.

"Priscilla," Alex said, his British accent lending a soft cadence to her name, "your music isn't just part of your world—it transforms the world of those who hear it. And you are not crazy; you're inspired. And inspiring."

His words washed over her, a balm to the sting of past rejections and self-doubt. Prissy took a deep breath, the air filling her lungs like the opening chord of a symphony—full of potential and anticipation.

"Look, I... I'm not good at this sorta thing," she admitted, her eyes flicking away for a moment before courage drew them back to his. "But whatever this is, between us... I want to explore it. With you. And that scares me half to death because it's not just about the music anymore, or business, or keeping this thing between us strictly platonic. I want you Alex, I want you."

The vulnerability in her declaration hung between them, delicate and unsteady as a vibrato on a high note. She was laying bare her soul, not just through her music now, but through the confession of her growing affection for him, an affection as nuanced and complex as the compositions she played. The fear of betrayal, of manipulation in their world of wealth and privilege, always loomed—but in that moment, with Alex, it seemed a risk worth taking.

Alex's expression softened, his eyes crinkling at the corners as a warm smile spread across his face. He took a step closer, his body angled toward her in a subtle expression of attentiveness and desire. Reaching out, he gently cupped her cheek, his thumb grazing the soft curve with a tenderness that belied his aristocratic exterior.

"Priscilla," he murmured, the single word carrying a world of affection. "You captivate me in ways I've never experienced before." His gaze held hers, intense yet grounding, a balm to the swirl of doubts and insecurities that so often plagued her. "Your talent, your passion, your spirit—they all move me in ways I cannot explain."

Prissy felt herself leaning into his touch, drawn to the sincerity and vulnerability he allowed her to witness. A shuddering breath escaped her lips as she lifted her hand to cover his, holding it against her cheek for a fleeting moment before threading their fingers together.

"Play for me?" he asked, his voice thick with emotion.

eleven

Priscilla's fingers danced across the strings, nimble and restless, plucking out the opening notes to tune her new cello. Her brow furrowed, lips pursed in concentration as a bead of sweat traced the curve of her cheek. This private performance for Alex meant everything - a chance to bare her soul through the haunting lilt of the cello's lament.

She inhaled deeply, willing her trembling hands to steady. *Get it together, Priss,* she thought, smoothing her palms along the sleek wooden curves. In this intimate salon, there was nowhere to hide, no orchestra to camouflage any errant notes or sour harmonies. Just her raw talent laid bare before his discerning British eyes.

With a final breath, Priscilla drew the bow across the strings in one sweeping motion. A mournful melody resonated through the hushed room, the notes hanging heavy with longing. She closed her eyes, losing herself in the visceral ache of every pluck and glissando. The cello's cry became an extension of her own heart's whispers, raw and exposed before Alex.

Each crescendo unleashed the storm of feelings she struggled to contain - the aching need, the dizzying lust, the wrestle between desire and dread of something so intoxicating. She poured it all into the strings, hips swaying with the driving rhythm as her fingers blurred across the fingerboard. If she couldn't find the words, the music would speak the depths of her craving for him.

The final, quavering note lingered in the air like a lover's sigh. Slowly, Priscilla's eyes fluttered open, her chest heaving. She felt deliciously undone yet achingly vulnerable before Alex's penetrating gaze.

Priscilla's fingers trembled ever so slightly as she lowered the bow, her dark eyes locking with Alex's across the dimly lit salon. The air seemed to thicken with an intangible tension, laden with the unspoken hunger her performance had laid bare.

Alex sat motionless in the plush leather armchair, transfixed. His piercing green eyes drank in every nuance of her movement, following the mesmerizing sway of her hips, the rise and fall of her chest. A muscle twitched along his chiseled jaw as his throat constricted with barely restrained desire.

"Brilliant..." he finally exhaled, his lyrical British lilt seeming to caress the solitary word. "Utterly brilliant, Priscilla."

A delicious shiver rippled through her at the unmistakable timbre of want underlying his praise. Heat blossomed across her brown skin as their gazes remained locked, twin confessions simmering in that charged silence.

The cello slipped from her slackened grip with a dolorous thump against the Persian rug. In the next breath, she was across the room, pulled forward by the irresistible force of his stormy eyes. Alex rose to his full towering height as she neared, his broad shoulders blocking out the low light.

"You play with such..." he rumbled, head dipping until his lips brushed the delicate whorls of her ear. "Passion."

A needy whimper escaped Priscilla's parted lips as his warm breath caressed her neck. Every nerve ending awakened with searing intensity, craving his slightest touch like a physical ache.

This... *this* was the crescendo she had been building toward, the primal hunger she could no longer deny.

Priscilla's fingers curled into the crisp linen of Alex's shirt, pulling him closer until the hard planes of his body pressed against the soft curves of her own. "You have no idea..." she murmured, her voice a low, velvet purr laced with unspoken promises.

One of Alex's hands trailed up the curve of her spine, his touch blazing through the thin material of her dress. He fisted a handful of those wild, ebony curls at her nape, tilting her head back to fully expose the elegant column of her throat. His hooded gaze drank in every inch of the offered expanse of velvety skin.

"Oh, but I think I do," he growled, the words a delicious rumble against the thundering pulse at her neck.

With agonizing slowness, he traced the path from her jaw to her collarbone with the barest graze of his lips, savoring the sharp intake of her breath. Priscilla's fingers flexed against the hard muscle of his back, nails raking through the fine material in silent encouragement.

She could smell the heady blend of his cologne, cedar and bergamot, mixed with the clean, masculine scent of his skin. It was an utterly intoxicating combination that made her head swim with wanting. The subtle rasp of his stubble against her sensitive skin was pure exquisite torture.

A low, guttural groan reverberated from deep within Alex's chest as he abruptly crushed his mouth against hers in a searing, demanding kiss. Priscilla melted into the onslaught, parting her lips in fervent invitation as their tongues met and danced in wild, heated exploration.

The room around them faded into a blissful blur as Priscilla and Alex lost themselves in their long-denied desire. Months of lingering glances and unspoken yearning meshed into an all-consuming hunger that demanded to be sated.

Priscilla's hands roamed the hard planes of Alex's back with greedy urgency, committing every ridge and valley to memory through her fingertips. His own calloused palms blazed a scorching trail down her sides, firmly mapping the lush curves concealed beneath the thin fabric.

She gasped sharply when his questing hands found the flare of her hips, thumbs pressing possessively into the softness there. "Alex..." His name tumbled from her lips, half-plea, half-prayer.

"Shh, love," he murmured against the corner of her parted mouth, voice husky with want. "Let me lavish you as you deserve."

Alex slammed Priscilla against the wall, devouring her mouth with a hunger that bordered on desperate. His hands roamed her curves, greedy for every inch of her luscious figure. Priscilla tugged at his shirt buttons, desperate to free his chocking cock from its constraints. Fabric rustled to the floor as they stripped each other of any barriers between them.

Priscilla's breath hitched when Alex's tongue laved her nipples, teasingly circling the hardened buds before sucking them into his warm mouth. She arched her back, offering more skin for him to explore. His strong hands cupped her ass cheeks, squeezing and kneading the supple flesh before dipping lower to discover her wetness. Priscilla moaned as his skilled digits explored her folds, teasing her swollen clit until she was trembling with desire. "Please," she whimpered, her voice hoarse with need.

Priscilla's body was aflame as Alex manipulated her sensitive flesh, his fingers delving deeper and pleasingly possessive. The cool touch of the wall against her heated skin was a stark contrast to the smoldering blaze that spread through her core. Hot kisses trailed down her neck, marking her as solely his.

Alex's lusty growl echoed around the room as he hoisted Priscilla effortlessly against the wall, her legs coiling instinctively around him. His throbbing arousal nestled at her entrance, its pulsating heat promising carnal fulfillment of the highest order.

"Tell me you want this," Alex demanded, a primal note resonating in his deep baritone voice. He pressed himself harder against Priscilla, causing her to gasp with unrefined anticipation. She met his gaze head-on, eyes glazed with ardor and desire, and affirmed in a husky tone she never knew she possessed, "Yes."

Time seemed to stand still as Alex entered Priscilla slowly, inch by shocking inch. Their breath hitched in unison at the exquisite connection their bodies shared. A guttural moan escaped from Alex's lips as he filled Priscilla entirely and felt the hot tightness of her clench around him.

Every dip and glide of his hips elicited whimpering panted pleas from Priscilla; a symphony of sounds and sighs echoing off the walls in perfect harmony with their rhythm. Lost in sensation, they drowned in each other's eyes - stormy greens colliding with dark pools of honey.

Priscilla began to move with him - undulating waves of motion against Alex's brute force. Her fingers clawed into his hard back as she sought purchase for leverage, increasing the pace until it became frenzied, desperate... wild.

Her pleasure soared, building momentum like an impending orchestra crescendo. Every pump sent shock waves of pleasure radiating through her entire body, culminating in a mind-numbing climax that had Priscilla's nails digging into Alex's back.

"Oh God, Alex..." Priscilla gasped, her voice barely above a whisper. His name was a benediction on her lips; the only coherent thought amidst the glorious chaos within.

Alex responded with a low groan, his hips pistoning against hers in an erratic rhythm as he neared his own peak. His release roared out of him like a freight train, rivulets of moisture coating their entwined bodies and marking her as his once more.

Slowly their rhythms synchronized –two hearts beating as one– their breaths gradually steadying and their limbs heavy with satisfaction. The cello lay abandoned on the Persian rug - its intimate melody replaced by the raw symphony of their love.

As they slowly came down from their erotic high, they found solace nestled within each other's arms. Their entangled bodies hummed with satisfaction; the sensual echoes of their lovemaking still lingering amidst the carnal wreckage.

"Come," he coaxed, taking her hand. "Lay down with me on the rug."

Prissy did what she was told and laid down with Alex, side by side, instantly falling within his arms. Her head rested against his chest, the rhythmic beating of his heart a soothing melody in her ear. In the tranquil aftermath of their passionate union, she felt a profound contentment wash over her.

With a tender smile, Alex traced his fingers along the curve of her back, his touch featherlight yet electrifying. "That was...sublime, love," he murmured, his posh British accent laced with wonder.

Prissy tilted her head up, meeting his reverent gaze with her own luminous eyes. "For real?" She chuckled softly, her rich alto tinged with a hint of that unmistakable Los Angeles sass. "Your accent always did drive me crazy."

Alex grinned, unfazed by her playful jab. He caressed her cheek, marveling at the warmth of her smooth ebony skin. "And your spirit captivates me, my passionate muse."

They held each other's gazes, a universe of unspoken emotions flowing between them. Prissy felt herself getting lost in the stormy depths of Alex's eyes, her heart swelling with a love she had never imagined possible.

"I never thought I could feel like this," she confessed in a hushed whisper. "You make me come undone in the best way."

His arms tightened around her, pulling her closer until their bodies melded seamlessly. "Nor I," he murmured against the crown of her head. "You've awoken something primal within me, Priscilla. Something I thought I'd lost long ago."

Prissy brushed her lips across his, then trailed down his neck with butterfly kisses. The act seemed to ignite something carnal within him and Alex laid his body over hers in a flash, paying homage to her breasts with his wicked mouth.

"Squirm for me, kitten," he growled sensually into her ear. The intoxicating mix of his British accent and the animalistic command sent shivers down Priscilla's spine.

"Make me purr then, tiger," she moaned, arching her back to offer herself even more to his delicious torment. He sucked harder on her nipple before switching to the other one, relishing in the way she writhed beneath him. The taste of her sweet skin drove him wild and only spurred him onward.

Her hand slipped downward, tracing a teasing path across his chiselled abs towards his expanding cock, thrusting towards her hand. "So fucking big," she purred salaciously. Her hand left his throbbing length and started exploring lower—to his balls. The coarse hairs tickled her fingertips as she gently massaged them, rolling them between her fingers while watching Alex's face contort in pleasure.

He groaned as she dared to touch him, her soft palm causing him to harden even more under her intimate caress. Desperate for more, he opened her legs wider with his own leg, pushing inside her. He kept one hand on her breast, his fingers dancing over her sensitive skin, while the other lifted her leg higher, deepening their connection. As they moved together, he couldn't help but marvel at the way her eyes widened with each thrust, her moans growing louder and more desperate. Her body quivered beneath his, and her cheeks flushed a rosy pink, a testament to their shared passion.

"Oh fuck," he growled as he started to pump in and out of her at a punishing pace, "You're so wet for me." The dirty words were delivered right against her earlobe in the same posh British accent she adored which only increased the raw heat simmering between them.

Her inner walls clenched around him instinctively, and she could hardly contain the whorls of pleasure washing over her. She met each of his powerful thrusts with one of her own, their bodies moving in sync like two well-practised dancers on a stage. As tension coiled tighter in her lower belly, Prissy knew she wouldn't last much longer.

"Harder, Alex...*harder*," she begged desperately, clawing at his back to bring him closer.

With a sinful grin, Alex grabbed her hips and adjusted his angle to hit that sweet spot inside her that elicited a loud cry from Prissy's lips while euphoric waves crashed through her senses.

twelve

The shrill ring of Prissy's phone shattered the hushed reverence of her practice space. She grimaced, plucking the device from her bag with slender fingers. An unknown number flashed on the screen.

"Yeah?" she answered, unable to mask her annoyance.

"Miss Alexander? Charlotte Hargreaves here. I apologize for the disruption, but I have an intriguing proposition that warrants your undivided attention."

Prissy's brow furrowed as she immediately recognized the clipped, authoritative British lilt. The infamous art maven's reputation preceded her – she moved with a ruthless single-mindedness in high society's inner circles.

"I'm listening..." Prissy replied, intrigue piquing despite herself.

"Marvelous. I'd like to discuss the matter in person, if you're amenable. Say, 3 o'clock at the Idelle Gallery?"

Prissy chewed her lip, debating. Finally, "I'll be there."

. . .

LATER THAT AFTERNOON, Prissy found herself in the sleek, chrome-accented gallery. The scent of money and privilege hung heavy amid the stark white walls displaying multimillion-dollar artworks.

A diminutive figure in a gunmetal grey skirt suit strode towards her, hand outstretched. "Miss Alexander, a pleasure." Lottie's grip was firm, her gaze appraising.

"Just call me Prissy," she replied cooly, matching the woman's brusque demeanor.

"Very well, Prissy. Shall we?" Lottie gestured towards a secluded sitting area. "I have an extraordinary opportunity that I believe will be an ideal vehicle for your...talents."

Prissy's defenses immediately rose as Lottie laid out her grand vision - a globetrotting multimedia showcase allowing Prissy's cello mastery to be exhibited like never before. The money, the exposure...it was staggering.

"So you see, this puts you on an international stage, my dear," Lottie purred. "You'd be utterly daft to refuse."

Prissy held Lottie's piercing gaze, her mind spinning with the grand opportunity laid before her.

VALIDATION.

TWO BIG BREAKS she's always dreamt of - a chance to bring her music to audiences around the world. Bigger and wider than Alex's vision ... The money, the prestige, the exposure...it was almost too much to comprehend.

Yet a nagging tendril of unease slithered through her. Something about Lottie's shark-like manner set her on edge. There was an underlying current of manipulation as if the woman was damned determined to sink her teeth into Prissy's career by any means necessary.

She shifted in the plush gallery seat. "And you will manage my career?"

Lottie smiled graciously, "That is part of the deal, yes. Exclusivity—with a 70-30 split."

Prissy hated talking numbers. *She never even spoke to Alex about his split!* "I...I'll have to think it over, Ms. Hargreaves. It's an incredible offer, no doubt. But I can't just decide something this major on the spot, is that OK?"

Lottie's thin lips pressed into a taut line, but she gave a curt nod. "Of course, of course. I suspected you'd need some time to mull it over. But don't dawdle overlong, dear. Opportunities like this are rare birds indeed."

The two women rose, Lottie extending her hand once more in an air of frosty finality. Prissy matched the firm grip, her uncertain gaze meeting the curator's predatory stare.

As she exited onto the street, Prissy felt a strange unraveling inside. Her head swam with the dizzying potential of Lottie's proposal...and the sobering reality that accepting it may mean leaving so much behind.

She wandered aimlessly for a few blocks before finding herself outside a cozy cafe, the aroma of freshly brewed coffee beckoning her inside. Ordering a large cappuccino, Prissy settled into a corner booth, cradling the comforting mug.

The rich, indulgent brew's first few sips did little to settle her reeling mind. Closing her eyes, she tried to ground herself, to unpack the tangled mess of thoughts and emotions.

On one hand, this was the big damn break she'd been hustling for, a chance to elevate herself from local virtuoso to global phenomenon. The kind of notoriety and finances that would allow her to finally chase her art with total freedom.

But the other side of the coin gave her pause. There was her blossoming...something...with the sophisticated and passionate Alex. She knew getting entwined with him, with his circles and spaces, would be complicated enough for a struggling artist like herself.

If she took Lottie's offer and left it all behind to jet-set across the globe, would the delicate buds of her and Alex's connection be able to survive? Or would the high-stakes opportunity sever those tenuous roots before they had a chance to fully blossom?

The cafe's door swung open, sending a cool breeze across Prissy's face. She looked up to see Alex stride in, eyes scanning the room until they locked onto hers. A warm smile spread across his charming British features as he made his way towards her corner nook.

"There you are, love," he said, sliding into the booth across from her. "I had a feeling I might find you pondering life's great questions over an exorbitantly overpriced coffee drink."

Prissy couldn't help but smirk at his playful jab, her heart fluttering at the casual endearment that rolled so naturally off his tongue. "You know me too well. Though I suppose this particular crisis calls for a hefty caffeine intake."

His brow furrowed with concern. "Something to do with that meeting earlier?"

"Yes," she breathed, continuing, "And before you say anything else. What is your split?"

Alex looked at her like she had three eyes in the center of her head. "Split?"

Prissy nodded her head, "Yes Alex, split. What commission did you intend on taking once the money starts coming in from **our** gig?"

Alex thought about it for a moment—*what was she fishing for? Hargreaves,* he knew in an instant. *That money-hungry hag.* "We never discussed money, love. But I would never do you a disservice when you are just starting out in your career. Is ten percent too much?"

Prissy's smile widened. "No, ten percent is just right."

"Now tell me all about your meeting, love," Alex coaxed, blowing her an air kiss.

Prissy sighed, giving a small nod as she cradled the warm mug between her palms. "Girl wants to whisk me away on some big-time global art tour. Talkin' major cash, massive exposure, the whole nine yards." She paused, chewing her lip. "The deal is on a larger scale than yours, Alex."

Her gaze drifted to meet his, those warm chocolate eyes filled with unvoiced worries. He knew Charlotte Hargreaves had deep pockets with noble connections—something he aspired for—which is where Priscilla comes in. Alex reached across the table, his palm sliding over her knuckles in a tender gesture. "I can only imagine how dizzying such an opportunity must feel," he said softly. "But you mustn't lose sight of your immense talent, Priscilla. You were born to captivate audiences with that brilliant mind and soul of yours."

A lump formed in her throat at his words, at the sincerity shining in his piercing green eyes. Here was a man who honestly seemed to believe in her more than she believed in herself sometimes. "Will you match her deal?"

Alex leaned back in his chair, his hand still covering hers in a reassuring warmth. "If a global tour is where your heart lies, then I'll be the first to help you get there."

But first, she'd have to commit to *his* tour, then start a global one. Prissy swallowed hard, tamping down the sudden ache in her chest at the thought of being separated from him - from this unexpected connection, they'd forged through music and shared vulnerability. "I don't wanna lose you, Alex," she confessed in a small voice. "What we've built together these past few months...it means everythin' to me."

Alex swallowed hard. She was contemplating Hargreaves offer, he knew so by the sound of her tone. If she really wanted to stay, they wouldn't be having this conversation. Prissy sounded like she wanted him to talk her out of it. She meant too much to him to hold her back—he had to let her fly.

His thumb stroked over her knuckles in a soothing caress. "And it means more to me than you could possibly fathom, love. But I don't want you shackling your brilliant wings for my sake." Alex's gaze was earnest, willing her to understand. "Your happiness, your fulfillment, is paramount. If that path diverges from mine for a spell, so be it. I'll still be here when you return, waiting with bated breath to hear the stories of how you dazzled the world."

A tremulous smile curved Prissy's lips at his unwavering faith in her. But that's not what she wanted to hear. She turned her palm up, lacing their fingers in a tight clasp as she searched the depths of those crystal green eyes. "You really don't mind? Puttin' us on hold like that while I go gallivantin' across the globe?"

Alex huffed a soft chuckle, leaning in conspirationally. "I'd be lying if I said the prospect doesn't sting, even just a bit. But my want for you, my admiration, runs far deeper than any selfish desire to keep you tethered at my side." His free hand drifted up to tuck an errant curl behind her ear. "Do what sets your soul ablaze, Priscilla. I'll be your safe harbor to return to when you've had your ravishing adventures."

Prissy pulled back, absently worrying her plump bottom lip between her teeth as she considered Alex's steadfast reassurance. She wanted to believe his serene acceptance came without strain, but the niggling fear that pursuing Lottie's tantalizing offer could irrevocably fracture the intimacy they'd built gnawed incessantly.

With a soft sigh, she extricated herself from his embrace and slipped off the overstuffed sofa. "I...I need to think on this, babe. Clear my head a bit." Prissy smoothed her palms down the soft cotton of her skirt, offering Alex an apologetic glance. "That cool?"

"Of course, my dear." The curator's lips curved in a tender

smile, his understanding plain. "Take all the time you require. I'll be here whenever you've settled your turbulent thoughts."

Nodding her thanks, Prissy turned on her heel and strode out the door of the cafe, pulling the door closed with a soft snick. She didn't envy the internal war Alex was undoubtedly waging - wanting her unbridled happiness while having to face the prospect of her temporary absence. The man's selfless devotion was as humbling as it was inspiring.

The cool night breeze gave her a moment's break as she strolled through the busy street. Prissy's thoughts raced, torn between two possibilities. One was a peaceful picture of staying with Alex, their creative passions entwined in harmony. The other was a vibrant scene filled with the excitement of international recognition and her music ignited audiences in a frenzy.

After wandering for what felt like an eternity, Prissy found herself sequestered in a quiet bus stop bench.

Her choice seemed painfully clear, whittled down to two divergent paths - either remain entrenched in the intimate warmth and security of what she'd cultivated with Alex...or step out into the great, untamed unknown Lottie so enticingly brought forth. With a rueful sigh, Prissy steadied her palms and allowed her eyelids to flutter close.

She opened her eyes with determination and knew where her loyalty lay - with the man who believed in her more than she believed in herself. He encouraged her to break through her limitations every day, and his unwavering love lifted her up during times of creative struggle.

Prissy walked down the sidewalk, her heels clicking against the pavement. The air was cold, but she felt determined. She approached the studio where she and Alex had spent so much time on their masterpiece, and her pace slowed.

There he was, silhouetted in the large window - bent over his easel with that intense furrow etched into his brow. Even from this distance, she could detect the tension coiled in the slopes of his shoulders, the tight line of his lips as he worked. A pang lanced through her chest. He was undoubtedly still agonizing over her potential exit.

Squaring her shoulders, Prissy pushed open the door and slipped inside. The smell of oils and turpentine enveloped her in a strangely comforting embrace. Alex startled at the sound, his brush clattering to the floor as he whirled to face her.

"Priscilla..." He breathed her name like a prayer, those piercing green eyes drinking her in with naked longing.

She held his gaze, letting the moment stretch out into a heavy anticipation. Then, without preamble, Prissy closed the distance between them in three long strides. Framing his face in her hands, she crashed her lips against his in a searing, hungry kiss.

Alex froze for the span of a heartbeat before melting into her with a groan, clutching her body flush against his own. Their mouths moved in a desperate, familiar dance - seeking, savoring, surrendering. When they finally broke apart, chests heaving, Prissy tenderly brushed an errant lock of chestnut hair from his brow.

"You, Alexander Shefton," she murmured, voice thick with a heady cocktail of desire and adoration. "Are the masterpiece I choose."

A slow, relieved smile curved his lips as understanding dawned. "Really, love? You're certain?"

Prissy nodded, resolute. "There ain't no gallery big enough to contain what we buildin' right here. I belong with you, babe."

Alex pulled her close, reveling in the sensation of their bodies pressed together. They embraced tightly, lost in a moment of intense connection and desire, the rest of the world fading away around them.

At length, Prissy drew back just enough to gaze up at him with those soulful, lambent eyes. "We both know this ain't gonna be no cakewalk though, right? Lottie and them artsy folks ain't gonna take kindly to me turnin' down that gig."

Alex somberly nodded. "You're likely correct, my darling. The backlash could be...severe, to say the least. We may find many doors closed to us, at least for a time."

Tucking a stray curl behind her ear, he held her face cradled in his palm with an intensity that stole her breath. "But I'll not have you compromise your truth for anything, Priscilla. Not for social cachet...not for coin...not even for your craft, as dear as it is to you. We'll weather whatever tempests may come, steadfast in our conviction."

Prissy felt her heart swell three sizes too large for her chest as she gazed upon this remarkable man - her partner, her champion, her insuppressible soul fire. Looping her arms around his neck, she pulled him down into another smoldering liplock.

"Then let the haters hate," she murmured against his lips with a soft, defiant chuckle. "We got everything we need right here, baby."

thirteen

Prissy stared vacantly at the wisps of smoke curling from the ashtray, her mind replaying Alex's words about Rafe's imminent departure. That suave Brit had a knack for casually dropping bombshells with his cultivated upper-crust lilt. She exhaled slowly, watching the smoke dissipate like Rafe's presence would soon vanish from the jazz club's dimly lit stage.

A hollow ache tugged at her chest. For years, she and Rafe had been a seamless musical duo, her cello's mournful lament intertwining with his guitar's fervent pleas. Without him, the synergy would crumble, scattering their devoted patrons. The thought of facing those empty chairs beside the stage made her shudder.

Rafe's leaving didn't just disrupt their performances - it chipped away at the unspoken bond they'd forged over countless jam sessions and post-gig drinks. With a disgruntled snort, Prissy stubbed out her cigarette and strode toward the club's backstage area.

The usually vibrant space was barren, instruments packed away and amp cords coiled like slumbering serpents. At the center stood Rafe, shoulders curved as he transferred his beloved guitar into its case with uncharacteristic resignation.

"So it's true?" Prissy's alto sliced through the stillness. "You bailin' on us, homeboy?"

Rafe glanced up, eyes glinting with a rueful smile. "Couldn't sneak off without that hawk-vision of yours spotting me, could I?"

Prissy crossed her arms, arching an eyebrow. "Don't play coy with me, Raf. Alex said you're taking your act elsewhere."

With a weary sigh, Rafe latched the guitar case. "It's time I spread these wings beyond our cozy little nest." His gaze drifted to the vacant stage. "Much as I'll miss setting this place on fire with you every night."

Prissy scowled, sauntering closer. "Damn right you'll miss it. We were magic up there, our groove tighter than a snare drum."

Rafe nodded solemnly. "No denying that, chica. But you know I can't stay boxed in here forever, as dope as our licks are." He straightened, a familiar glint rekindling in his eyes. "There's a whole world of crazy jazz cats to jam with, festivals to slay, record deals to chase down."

"So you aiming to be the next Wes Montgomery or something?" Prissy arched an eyebrow. "Getting delusions of grandeur, are we?"

Rafe flashed that roguish grin that made groupies swoon. "Hey, a man's gotta have ambitions, right? I'm too talented to just kick it in this one little club til I'm old and arthritic."

Prissy sucked her teeth derisively. She hated to admit it, but he was right - his skills were too prodigious to squander indefinitely. Still, the thought of severing their dynamite musical kinship stung like an improvised jazz solo hitting a sour note.

"I get it," she relented. "You wanna go make your mark, be a bigshot guitar slinger. Just don't be expecting me to come groveling for you to grace my stage when you make it huge."

Rafe barked a laugh, clapping her on the shoulder

affectionately. "As if I could ever find a cellist who vibes with me like you do, Priss. We were destined to reunite, no matter where this crazy muse takes us."

A wistful smile played across Prissy's lips as their eyes met, a whole unspoken conversation flowing between them. She was really going to miss this idiot.

Prissy sighed heavily, shifting her weight. As much as she hated to admit it, she understood Rafe's drive to spread his wings. Hell, she'd felt those same burning ambitions all her life - to stamp her mark on the music world, to etch her name among the greats.

"I ain't gonna try and stop you from chasing your dreams, Rafe," she said, her voice taking on a softer edge. "You got a gift, and gifts like that are meant to be shared with the world, not kept cooped up in one little jazz joint."

She reached out, giving his arm a firm squeeze. "You go on and do your thing, kid. Break on through to the other side and all that. Just don't forget the little people when you make it big."

A teasing smirk played across her lips, but her eyes shone with sincerity. As much as she dreaded the void his absence would leave, she wanted nothing more than for him to soar.

Rafe's cocksure grin melted into a Look of surprised gratitude. He covered her hand with his own, holding her gaze intently.

"You know I could never forget you, Prissy," he said earnestly. "My music wouldn't be half what it is without your spirit breathing life into it up there on stage. We're a team - now and always."

He pulled her into a fierce embrace, his sculpted arms enveloping her petite frame. Prissy tensed initially, then relaxed into the hug, giving his back an affectionate pat.

When they parted, Rafe's eyes danced with their usual mischief. "Who knows? Maybe I'll get so stinking rich and famous that I can hire you as my personal accompanist."

Prissy rolled her eyes, failing to hide her grin. "You wish, hotshot. How 'bout when I get stinking rich and famous I will hire YOU as my personal accompanist?!"

They both laughed, the melancholy of the moment lifting momentarily. Because no matter what paths diverged before them, their connection through music would forever bind their spirits as one.

Prissy's gaze drifted to the empty stage, a pang of nostalgia tightening her chest. So many evenings spent under those warm lights, her cello crooning soulful melodies as Rafe's dexterous fingers danced across the strings. The jazz club had become their second home – a sanctuary where they could shed their inhibitions and lose themselves in the magic they created together.

Her mind drifted back to that open mic night years ago when their paths first crossed. She was a timid newcomer to the city, clutching her cello like a lifeline. Rafe, already a local favorite, had sauntered over with that roguish grin, inviting her to join his impromptu jam session. From the first note, something electric had sparked between them, their contrasting styles converging into a harmonious rapture.

Countless performances followed, each one a journey of self-discovery. Rafe's fiery passion had ignited her own flames, coaxing her out of her shell and teaching her to embrace the raw vulnerability of her art. In turn, her musical elegance had grounded his frenetic energy, weaving intricate tapestries upon which he could freely improvise.

Together, they had weathered the storms – those nights when the muse eluded them, when doubt crept in like a venomous serpent. But they had always emerged victorious, their bond fortified by the shared struggle and eventual triumph.

Now, as the prospect of that chapter closing loomed before her, Prissy found herself awash in a bittersweet ache. She would miss the thrill of their musical trysts, the way their souls intertwined with every crescendo and diminuendo. Yet, she knew in her heart that Rafe's boundless spirit could never be contained within these four walls forever.

Turning to face him, she saw the restless fire burning in his eyes – a fire she had stoked and nurtured but could never tame. With a melancholic smile, she gave his hand a gentle squeeze, a silent vow to always cherish the indelible mark he had left on her life's melody.

"Rafe," Prissy began, her velvet voice caressing his name like a cherished refrain. "These years performing together have been the greatest gift. You helped me find the courage to bare my soul through my music."

She paused, lips pursed as a kaleidoscope of memories danced behind her eyes – their first tentative duet, the standing ovations that followed, the countless after-show drinks where they dissected every note until last call.

"You've been my muse, my partner in crime on this crazy musical journey," she continued, chuckling softly. "But I know your talents were meant for bigger stages. As much as I'll miss you by my side, I'll be cheering you on from the front row."

Rafe's throat constricted with a swell of emotion he couldn't quite name. This woman, with her regal poise and depth of feeling, had seen him at his most vulnerable – stripped bare before the altar of music. A fraternal bond had blossomed between them, an unspoken language forged in the fires of their creative passions.

Clearing his throat, he met her gaze with an intensity that belied the casual sweep of his tousled curls. "Chica, you gave this lost soul a home and a purpose. Your grace, your unwavering belief in me...it's what kept me going all these years."

A wistful smile played upon his lips as he reached out, calloused fingertips grazing her cheek in a tender caress. "No matter where this crazy ride takes me, you'll always be the one who showed me the true power of music – to heal, to transcend, to forge connections that can never be broken."

Prissy leaned into his touch, savoring the warmth and the solidity of his presence one last time. Though the road diverged here, she knew their spirits would forever remain entwined by the ethereal melodies they had woven together.

"We'll find our way back to each other someday," she murmured, a promise sealed with the secrets only soulmates could share. "This isn't goodbye, Rafe – it's just the next movement in our symphonic journey."

With a tender smile, Prissy stepped forward and wrapped her arms around Rafe's broad shoulders, embracing him tightly. She breathed in the familiar scent of sandalwood and sweat that clung to his worn leather jacket, a comforting reminder of the countless nights they had shared the stage together.

Rafe's arms enveloped her slender frame, his calloused fingers pressing into the curve of her back as he returned the embrace with equal fervor. In that moment, the world around them seemed to fade away, leaving only the steady beat of their hearts and the lingering echoes of the music they had poured their souls into.

Prissy nodded, blinking back the tears that threatened to spill onto her cheeks. She knew that their bond transcended mere physical proximity, a testament to the power of their art to forge unbreakable ties. With a steadying breath, she allowed the melancholic melody of their farewell to swell within her, trusting that it would one day give way to a harmonious reunion.

"Until then," she whispered, offering Rafe a watery smile, "may the music guide your path and bring you all the success you deserve."

Rafe returned her smile with a roguish grin, his eyes crinkling at the corners. "And may it lead us back to each other when the time is right, *mi alma gemela*."

fourteen

The mahogany cello groaned in agony, its melancholic voice swelling against the soundproofed walls. Prissy's fingers danced maddeningly across the strings, coaxing forth the haunting melody that had eluded her for weeks. A bead of sweat trickled down her furrowed brow as she lost herself in the throes of artistic torment. *Damn this infernal passage!* Her bow trembled, the sorrowful notes fracturing like shards of splintered glass.

A sharp rap at the door shattered her trance. Prissy startled, the cello's mournful cry abruptly silenced. She whipped around, chest heaving with frustration and dark curls misting across her flushed cheeks.

The door creaked open to reveal Alex's towering frame, impeccably adorned in a crisp linen suit. "Am I interrupting something, love?" His smooth baritone sliced through the lingering dissonance.

Prissy's eyes narrowed at the endearment. "What do you want, Alex?" She couldn't mask the annoyance edging her tone, though curiosity flickered beneath her scowl.

He raised his hands in mock surrender. "Easy now, just

thought I'd pop by and see how rehearsals are coming along." Alex's gaze raked over the chaos of sheet music strewn about her like fallen leaves. "Though it appears my timing is...inopportune."

Alex sauntered into the practice room, hands casually tucked in his pockets as he surveyed the space with a critical eye. "That last run wasn't half bad, but your bowing could use a bit more...finesse."

He demonstrated an exaggerated up-bow motion, his cocksure smile grating on Prissy's last nerve. She ground her teeth, the cello protesting with a dull thrum as her knuckles tightened around the neck.

"I don't recall asking for your input," she bit out, dark eyes flashing dangerously.

Alex arched an immaculately groomed brow. "Come now, no need to get your knickers in a twist, love. I'm only trying to help guide that raw talent of yours."

His patronizing tone was like sandpaper against her pride. Prissy rose to her full height, back ramrod straight as she clutched the cello possessively. "Guide me? You mean dictate and micromanage every bloody note!" She could no longer filter the torrent of grievances bubbling up from the depths of her frustrations. "This is my music, Alex! My emotions were laid bare for the world to hear. I don't need you steamrolling over my artistry with your insufferable critiques and arbitrary standards!"

Alex's jaw tightened, cool eyes glinting like steel. When he spoke, his words were dangerously soft. "Is that so? Need I remind you whose connections secured this debut in the first place? You'd be dossing around playing vacant pubs if not for me taking a gamble on your...unrefined talents."

The barb struck deep, peeling away at the brittle layers of her self-doubt. Prissy flinched, hating how his condescending tone could still claw at her insecurities. She rallied her resolve, lifting her chin in defiant challenge.

"Then it seems we've reached an impasse. I cannot perform under your totalitarian direction any longer." Her voice was steady, solid as an ancient oak refusing to be swayed by the gales. "This is my music, my life's opus, and I'll play it on my own terms."

The crisp click of the door punctuated the tense silence as Alex swept out without another word. Prissy sank onto the worn sofa, cradling her cello like a child clutching a tattered doll for comfort. Alone at last, the adrenaline drained from her veins, leaving a hollowness that felt sickeningly familiar.

She traced the elegant curves of the instrument, mind drifting back to that pivotal night when her world shattered into splinters of dissonance. The soaring melodies, the thunderous applause...all crumbling to ashes under the stark lights and hushed whispers backstage. "You have amazing talent, but is classical really...appropriate for someone like you?"

Prissy shuddered, fingers digging into the lacquered wood as waves of self-doubt crashed over her. Alex's biting words reverberated through her mind - was she really just an "unrefined talent" playing make-believe at being a true artist? Despite all her years of study, the rigorous practice, could she ever escape being seen as that girl from the wrong side of the tracks?

A muffled buzzing jolted her from the turbulent reverie. Prissy fished her phone out, chest constricting at Alex's name flashing on the screen. She almost declined the call, but something in her quivered at the thought of that unbridgeable chasm yawning between them.

"Prissy..." His cultured voice caressed her name with uncharacteristic tenderness. "I'm afraid I was an arrogant prick earlier. You're the paragon of artistry, not some protege to be molded by my insipid ramblings."

Prissy held her breath, the apology as unexpected as a winter blossom unfurling in the snow. Alex's tone softened further, regret palpable.

"Your music is brilliant, simply brilliant. And you..." He paused, as if tasting the weight of the words. "You're the most exquisite, passionate woman I've ever known. I want nothing more than to see you shine on that stage, my brilliant crimson monarch."

A treacherous lump formed in her throat at the heartfelt endearment. This was the Alex who first entranced her - the refined gentleman hiding an ardent romantic behind his cultivated airs. Her chest ached with longing to trust his velvet words, to revel in the warmth of his belief in her talents.

Prissy clutched the phone tighter as conflicting emotions swirled within her. Part of her yearned to surrender to Alex's honeyed apology, to let the soothing balm of his adoration wash over her frayed nerves. His fervent avowal rekindled the spark that first drew her to this sophisticated man who seemed to prize her art above all else.

Yet a voice nagged from the recesses of her mind, a dissonant chord amidst the harmonious refrain of his contrition. Hadn't she felt this intoxicating rush before, only to have it curdled by his relentless need to orchestrate every beat of her life? Brutal memories resurfaced of him berating her interpretation, condescendingly lecturing on the "proper" way to imbue the music with emotion.

As if he, for all his cultured pretensions, could fathom the depths from which she drew her passion!

Prissy worried her bottom lip, scrambling to un-riddle the perplexing tangle of her feelings. She loved this man, truly loved the side of him that cherished her fierce artistry. But could she endure another descent into the maelstrom of his control? The exhibit loomed like a gilded cage, where even her greatest triumph would be decked in his ornate visions.

Was it just nerves?!

A muted rapping came from the living room. Prissy hastily

mumbled something about calling Alex back and hustled to the door.

Her sister Miriam stood smiling in the hallway, two-year-old Jayla perched on her hip. "Hey sis, thought I'd stop by and–" Miriam's sunny expression clouded as she took in Prissy's troubled countenance. "Damn, what's got you lookin' like somebody stomped on your favorite Cellie cello?"

Prissy swallowed hard. Always the perceptive one, her sister could decrypt her most inscrutable moods with a glance. She ushered them inside, sinking onto the couch as Miriam deposited Jayla amid a flurry of toys.

"It's...it's Alex," she finally said, struggling to find the words. Revealing the fissures in their relationship made them feel profoundly, inescapably real. "He called, apologizing for how he acted earlier. Saying all these sweet things about believing in me and my talents." She exhaled shakily. "But I don't know if I can trust it, Miri. He's been so controlling lately, trying to dictate how I should play, like he knows my music better than I do."

Miriam's eyes softened with sympathy as she settled beside Prissy. "Aw, baby girl. I know how much you've been stressin' over this whole showcase thing." Her hand found Prissy's, giving it an affectionate squeeze. "But you listen to me now - ain't nobody who can play like you when you're in that zone, okay? You was born to make music, and anybody with working ears can hear that."

A tremulous smile played across Prissy's lips at her sister's fierce belief. Miriam was her stalwart champion, the one who rallied her spirits when self-doubt crept in like an insidious malady.

"I just...I worry if I'm good enough for this," she confessed in a small voice. "What if Alex is right, and I'm not playing it 'properly'?" She made air-quotes with her fingers. "What if I choke out there in front of everyone? All those hoity-toity art snobs scrutinizing my every note."

"Then screw 'em!" Miriam said with a disarming bluntness that made Prissy's eyes go wide. "Look, you got yourself one chance at this exhibit, right? So why don't you go out there and show those pompous asses what real music sounds like?"

Prissy couldn't help but chuckle at her sister's trademark candor. Miriam had an uncanny ability to deflate any scenario down to its unvarnished essence.

"You're one hell of a cellist, Priss," Miriam continued, shifting closer until their shoulders brushed. "Own that shit, you hear? Don't let nobody make you second-guess your gift, not even Moneybags McGee with his hoity British butt." She nudged Prissy playfully. "Just say the word, and I'll go full *Married...with Children* on his scrawny ass."

Although Prissy was still nervous, she found herself feeling uplifted by Miriam's quick wit and unwavering devotion. Her sister had a talent for chasing away any doubts or insecurities, reminding Prissy of the simple joy she found in her art. Taking a deep breath, she pushed away her uncertainties and let the joyful melodies of an imaginary concerto drown out Alex's well-intentioned but suffocating critiques.

When the time came, she would play. Not to fulfill someone else's ideals, but to unleash the wild, passionate symphony that had always roared through her very bones.

THE NEXT AFTERNOON found Prissy sitting across from Alex at a secluded corner table in their favorite cafe. Fragrant espresso wafted between them, mingling with the faint strains of jazzy piano tinkling from the speakers. Despite the cozy ambiance, a palpable tension crackled in the air, matching the nervous flutter in Prissy's chest.

She took a grounding sip of her macchiato, letting the rich bitterness coat her tongue before meeting Alex's serious regard. "I need you to hear me out on this," she began, her voice low but resolute. "What happened yesterday..." She paused, chewing her full lip. "It can't happen again. Not like that."

Alex's posture stiffened imperceptibly, but he inclined his head. "Go on."

Prissy swirled the dregs in her cup, marshaling her thoughts. "This exhibit, my performance, it's the biggest opportunity of my career so far. But it's also deeply personal for me. The pieces I've chosen, the way I interpret them..." She raised her warm brown eyes to his cool green gaze. "It all comes from a private place, Alex. When you try to micromanage how I express that, it cheapens the whole thing. It makes me feel like you don't trust my artistry."

A muscle worked in Alex's chiseled jaw as he processed her words. At length, he exhaled a rueful sigh. "Bugger. You're right, I've been a bit of a controlling *prat*, haven't I?" His expression softened with contrition. "Force of habit, I suppose. In my circles, things are so choreographed, so precisely managed down to the finest detail. I've gotten accustomed to..."

"Dictating how things should be?" Prissy supplied, arching one finely sculpted brow.

Alex's lips twitched in a self-deprecating smirk. "Precisely. Dreadful tendency, I'm afraid. One I must endeavor to rectify going forward, as your partner." His eyes roamed her face with naked adoration. "Your talent, your passion, your brilliant effervescence on stage...it's why I fell for you in the first place, love. I never meant to diminish that radiance, only to support and refine it."

Prissy felt her cheeks warming at his ardent words, even as skepticism furrowed her brow. "You say that, but then I worry you'll just revert to old habits, start nitpicking and steamrolling my decisions again. I need breathing room to create on my own terms, Alex. I need to know you'll give me that space, that...that trust." Her voice wavered with raw vulnerability on the last word.

Alex reached across the table, his long fingers curling gently around her wrist. "I understand, love. Truly. And you have my solemn vow, I shall bridle my controlling impulses from this point forward." His green gaze bored into hers with an intensity that stole her breath. "This is your moment, your aria to shine. I'll be your patron, your champion...but also your respectful admirer, content to behold your transcendent gift from the crowd."

As Prissy gazed back at the man she loved, she felt the vice of trepidation loosening around her heart. She knew the path ahead would be arduous, haunted by the specter of their clashing creative visions. But Alex's words rang with sincerity and a willingness to adapt, to allow her the autonomy she craved. With that glimmer of trust binding them, perhaps they could walk that path together after all, in harmony instead of dissonance.

Prissy felt a swell of affection and newfound hope as she studied Alex's earnest expression. Though doubts still lingered, she chose to embrace the olive branch he extended, to believe in his commitment to change. With a tender smile, she turned her hand over, lacing her fingers through his.

"Alright, Mr. Shefton. I'll hold you to that vow." A playful glint danced in her warm brown eyes. "But fair warning, I'm a tough taskmaster when it comes to admiring audiences."

The corners of Alex's mouth quirked upward in that roguish grin she adored. "I relish the challenge, Miss Alexander."

fifteen
NEW YORK ART GALLERY EXHIBITION

REHEARSAL

The dimly lit hallway was quiet and still as Prissy practiced in one of the dressing rooms. Her skilled fingers glided along the cello's strings, creating melancholic melodies that echoed through the space. She worked up a sweat with determination, focusing on perfecting each note. Though her nerves were tense, she refused to give in. This was her chance to shine.

The rusty hinges of the door groaned, forcing Prissy to tear her eyes away from her cello. Alex, with his confident gait and perfectly tailored suit, sauntered into the room. She couldn't help but notice how the fabric hugged every curve of his athletic body. The corners of his mouth lifted into a charming smile as he studied her with intense, verdant-colored eyes. It took all of Prissy's willpower not to squirm under his penetrating gaze.

"Looking ravishing as ever, my raven-tressed virtuoso," he purred in that plummy timbre that always made her shiver. "Though your talents extend far beyond mere aesthetics on this propitious evening."

Prissy swallowed hard, mouth suddenly dry as the Sahara. "You flatter me, Alex. But I won't deny my hands are shakin' like leaves in a tornado right about now."

He tsked softly, closing the distance between them with two languid strides. Crouching before her, he cupped her trembling fingers in his warm palms, holding her gaze with scorching intensity. "This illustrious occasion marks your apex, darling. You were born to make the angels weep with rapture on that hallowed stage. Once we conquer America darling, we will surely vanquish Europe."

His proximity overwhelmed her senses with his rich, earthy cologne. She searched those fathomless eyes for any trickery, any artifice, yet found only adoration shimmering back at her. "You really believe in me that much, don't you?"

"I believe you hung the moon and stars themselves," he murmured. "Now seize your destiny with both hands and let that sublime talent blaze forth."

Alex's thumb caressed the back of Prissy's hand in a tender rhythm. "You are an artiste of the highest caliber, my love. This grand performance is merely the world's chance to behold what I've always seen - raw, unbridled genius."

Prissy's chest swelled with a mix of trepidation and affirmation. This British aristocrat with his honeyed words and penetrating gaze saw something in her that blazed brighter than any spotlight.

She licked her lips, tasting the salty remnants of her frayed nerves. "I want this night to be...for us. To play from the deepest wellspring of our journey together - the joy, the heartache, the passion."

A flicker of surprise crossed Alex's chiseled features before melting into a tender smile. "My dearest Priscilla, you never cease to astonish me." He brought her knuckles to his lips in a reverent kiss. "Unleash the full force of your emotion through your sublime gift. Let the world bear witness to the profound depths of our love."

Prissy's breath hitched at the devotion burning in his eyes. With Alex's ardor fortifying her, the doubts withered away like frost under a blazing sun. In this moment, she was invincible, an artistic force of nature.

Leaning forward, she brushed her full lips ever so lightly against his. "For us," she whispered, the mantra now seared into her soul. Rising with renewed poise, she collected her cello and made her stately way towards the wings, every step purposeful, regal - as befitting the queen about to claim her throne.

Prissy's fingers danced across the taut strings, coaxing forth a rich, melancholic melody that seemed to emanate from the very depths of her being. Each note she played was imbued with the turbulent emotions of their passionate affair - the rapturous highs, the aching lows, the desperate longing that had threatened to consume them both.

The cello sang their story, its haunting refrain weaving through the dimly lit backstage area like tendrils of smoke. Prissy's eyes were shut, lost in the music, her body swaying with the ebb and flow of the piece she had chosen to dedicate to their love.

Alex watched her, utterly transfixed, a maelstrom of pride and desire roiling within him. He drank in the sight of her - the graceful arch of her neck, the delicate flutter of her lashes, the way her lips parted ever so slightly as she coaxed forth each soulful note. In that moment, she was more than just his lover, his muse - she was a conduit for the very essence of artistry itself.

As the final, quavering note faded into silence, Prissy opened her eyes, her gaze instantly finding Alex's. A wordless exchange passed between them, a silent understanding that transcended mere language. This performance would be a declaration, a defiant cry against the forces that had sought to keep them apart, a testament to the unbreakable bond they shared.

Prissy rose, cradling her cello with reverence, and made her way towards Alex. Her steps were purposeful, unhurried, every movement radiating a quiet confidence born of her newfound resolve.

"Well?" she murmured, her voice a husky caress against the pulsing silence. "What do you think?"

Alex's throat worked as he struggled to find the words to encapsulate the maelstrom of emotions that threatened to overwhelm him. Finally, he simply shook his head in wonder. "Bloody brilliant, as always, my love," he rasped, his aristocratic veneer slipping in the face of such raw, unvarnished artistry.

Reaching out, he cupped her face in his palm, his thumb tracing the fine curve of her cheekbone. "You'll bring the house down," he declared, his voice ringing with absolute conviction. "And when you do, just know that I'll be there, in that audience, my heart swelling with pride..."

His gaze smoldered, equal parts adoration and white-hot desire. "...for the most extraordinary woman I've ever known."

Alex drew Prissy closer, until their bodies were flush against one another, the cello a sleek barrier between them. His scent – that heady amalgam of expensive cologne, fine whiskey, and the faintest hint of Cuban cigar smoke – enveloped her in its intoxicating spell.

Alex's hands roamed her body, stroking her hair, then tracing down her cheek, lingering on her neck and finally settling on her waist. The heat of his touch sent shivers down her spine and she could feel her nipples harden under the weight of her gown.

Her eyes met his, and the intensity of the connection sent a jolt of desire straight to her core. She could see the desire mirrored in his eyes, a hunger that matched her own. Prissy's lips parted slightly as she breathed in his scent, the intoxicating blend of cologne, whiskey, and cigar smoke making her head spin.

She felt the cello between them, a silken barrier of sorts, yet it only served to heighten the anticipation. The music filled the air, its melody swirling around them like a passionate dance. Their hands found each other, fingers intertwining, and a low hum of pleasure emanated from deep within her throat as she felt his strong hand tighten around hers.

Their bodies pressed closer, the heat of their skin merging as one. Alex's hand moved lower, sliding over her waist and down to her hip, his touch electrifying her with its force. Prissy's breath caught in her throat as she felt the ache between her legs grow, the desire building with every stroke of his hand.

Alex's fingers initiated a delicate dance along Prissy's silhouette, tracing the path from her silk-clad shoulder toward the provocative curve of her hip. His touch was like molten honey, slow and warm, sparking an inferno that seemed to consume them both.

The trace of his hand over her rosy peaks caused shivers to traverse down her spine, igniting dimples of pleasure that prickled against the lacy fabric of her gown. A moan escaped from her parted lips as she felt Alex's steely arousal press against the softness of her stomach. The sensation triggered a powerful throb within her core - a reminder of their shared need for intimacy.

"Mine," he growled into her ear – a promise that sent a hot wave of anticipation flooding through her veins. His fingertips danced lower, dipping beneath the hemline of her skirt to stroke the smooth expanse of thigh hidden there. It wasn't just touch, it was possession—an electrifying assertion of his claim on her body that had Prissy gasping for breath.

His nimble fingers found their way through the silk and lace, gently exploring the velvety heat nestled between her thighs. She squirmed under his attention, each stroke eliciting gasps and needy whimpers as he discovered every inch of her hidden treasure. "Open up for me, love," Alex husked out, his voice thick with desire as he prodded at the wet folds seeking entry.

A strangled cry left Prissy's lips as Alex plunged two digits into her slick heat. Her walls clenched around him in welcome, pulling him deeper while their tongues danced a lascivious duet mirroring their lower bodies' actions.

She broke away from their sinful kiss to throw back her head; exposing the graceful curve of her neck to his hungry gaze. A triumphant groan echoed in the room as Alex began to pump his fingers in a rhythm designed to wreck her senses. "That's it, love," he murmured, watching the pleasure contort her face. "Let go for me..."

His thumb moved to circle her swollen nub, adding fuel to the fire already ignited within Prissy. The pressure was exquisite, a maddening combination of lust and need that had every nerve ending in her body screaming for release.

The climax struck without warning, waves of pleasure that rippled down from her core to her trembling limbs. Each convulsion wrung another moan from Prissy's lips as she rode out the aftershocks of ecstasy. When she finally came back down to earth, Alex's heated gaze remained locked onto hers - a promise of more sinful delights to come.

sixteen

SHOW

The velvet curtain slowly parted, and Prissy stepped out onto the grand stage, cello in hand. Her heart hammered against her ribs as the blinding spotlight enveloped her in its brilliant glow. Rows upon rows of upturned faces gazed at her, eyes glittering with hushed anticipation.

Prissy swallowed hard, adjusting the bow in her trembling fingers. *Get it together. You've done this a thousand times before.* But this wasn't just any performance - it was the career-defining prelude to the international exhibit she had worked her entire life for. One wrong note, one slip of concentration, and it would all come crashing down.

She closed her eyes momentarily, inhaling a deep, steadying breath. The acrid scent of bone-dry rosin filled her nostrils. When she opened her eyes again, her chin lifted with renewed poise and determination.

With a fluid, practiced motion, Prissy drew the bow taut across the strings. The mournful wail of the cello sliced through the suffocating silence, its resonant vibrations pulsing through her very bones. She surrendered herself fully to the haunting melody, letting the swell of emotion pour forth unchecked.

The audience seemed to hold its collective breath, utterly bewitched. Prissy was no longer aware of their scrutinizing gazes - she existed solely within the intimacy of her art, coaxing forth its sublime beauty one impassioned note at a time. This was what she lived for.

Prissy lost herself in the ebb and flow of the music, her fingers dancing across the strings with effortless precision. The mournful notes swelled and resonated through the grand venue, wrapping the enraptured audience in their somber embrace.

Sweat dripped down her face as she poured her heart out through the intense performance. The cello seemed like a part of her, every shaky note a raw display of the inner turmoil and joy she felt. The melodies grew stronger, reaching a peak before falling into a stunned hush. Prissy's chest rose and fell with each straining breath, her fingers still shaking from the immense emotion she had put into every sweet tune.

Then, the spell broke with a collective indrawn breath. A solitary sniffle echoed through the hushed auditorium, swiftly followed by a rumbling torrent of thunderous applause. The ovation swelled into a deafening roar of approval as audience members shot to their feet, hands stinging from the fervor of their clapping.

Tears shined on many faces as they watched Prissy's performance. The raw emotion in her music caused a wave of cathartic sobs to spread through the audience. Overwhelmed by the response, Prissy stood and reveled in the love and praise from her fans. This was what she lived for - when her music connected her soul with those of her listeners.

No sooner had she stepped into the wings than a veritable stampede engulfed her. Well-wishers and admirers surged forward, a kaleidoscope of gushing smiles and outstretched hands. Esteemed critics grasped her fingers in their gnarled grips, eyes shining with reverence.

"Sublime, my dear! An absolute revelation!"

"You have singlehandedly elevated the cello to high art."

"I was transported, utterly spellbound from the first exquisite note."

Prissy flushed crimson under the torrent of effusive praise, murmuring modest thanks even as her chest swelled with pride. She had gambled everything on this pivotal performance - her reputation, her future prestige and earning potential. And it had paid off in spades, if the awe-struck faces surrounding her were any indication.

Her gaze flitted anxiously through the crush of admirers, searching for one face in particular. *Where was he?* Panic seized her - *surely he hadn't missed it?* Her heart thundered with a strange amalgam of desperate longing and queasy nerves.

At last, she spotted him across the teeming crowd, standing apart with an inscrutable look etched on those aristocratic features. Their eyes locked through the mass of bodies, and Prissy's breath caught in her throat.

There it was - the blazing look of pride and pure, undisguised desire that caused tremors down her spine. As Alex's gaze raked over her, devouring every inch of her sweat-sheened curves with carnal intensity, Prissy felt a delicious shiver tingle across her sensitized skin.

His hands moved in decisive, measured strokes, bringing them together in crisp, unhurried applause. But the smoldering admiration kindling in those verdant eyes spoke louder than any ovation. Prissy's core clenched with a fierce spike of want that left her weak in the knees.

Prissy began weaving her way through the thicket of well-wishers, her eyes locked on the magnetic pull of Alex's smoldering gaze. Bodies parted before her like the Red Sea, voices raised in raucous accolades falling on deaf ears. Nothing else mattered in that moment except reaching him.

As she drew nearer, the corners of Alex's lips quirked upwards in a rakish grin. His eyes danced with undisguised appreciation, hungrily drinking in every sway of her hips.

"Bloody brilliant, love," he murmured, arms encircling her in a searing embrace. The rich, smoky scent of his cologne clouded Prissy's senses as she melted against the solid wall of his chest. "You were transcendent up there."

A delighted shiver coursed through her at the rumbling timbre of his voice, the heated proximity of his body. "You really think so?" she breathed, basking in his ardent worship.

Alex's fingers traced feather-light patterns along her spine, igniting trails of gooseflesh. "I could scarcely breathe, enraptured by the raw talent you poured into every soulful note." His lips brushed the delicate whorls of her ear, sending molten lava searing through her veins. "You're a bloody virtuoso, my sweet."

Prissy flushed, equal parts thrilled and abashed by the smoldering intensity of his praise. "I couldn't have done it without your unwavering support," she confessed, nuzzling her cheek against the reassuring strength of his shoulder.

With a roguish wink, Alex slipped an arm around her waist, guiding her towards a secluded alcove. "I daresay this calls for a drink to celebrate, wouldn't you agree?" He snagged two flutes of fizzing champagne from a passing tray. "A toast - to the most captivating musician this side of the Atlantic." His eyes danced with playful challenge as he clinked his glass against hers. "And to making every risk utterly worthwhile."

After clinking glasses, Prissy took a fortifying sip of the

effervescent champagne, its bubbles tingling on her tongue. She drew a steadying breath, her grip tightening ever so slightly on the delicate crystal stem.

"Alex," she began, her voice dropping to an intimate murmur laced with nervous anticipation. "This night has been...magical. More than I ever could have dreamed." Worrying her lower lip, she searched his aristocratic features, those piercing green eyes holding her transfixed. "But I don't want it to end when the curtain falls."

One elegant brow arched in intrigued curiosity. "Oh? And what did you have in mind, love?"

Heat blossomed in her cheeks, but she pressed on with a courage she didn't quite feel. "Move in with me." The words tumbled out in a breathless rush. "Make this—us—permanent."

Alex went utterly still, his grip slackening until the champagne flute tilted precariously. "Prissy..." He exhaled a harsh breath, surprise and something deeper flickering across his chiseled features.

Her heart stuttered, panic clawing at her throat as she braced for rejection. But then his eyes softened, melting with an unmistakable warmth. Reaching out, he cupped her cheek with his free hand, callousing from years of playing guitar grazing her skin.

"You daft woman," he chided, the roughened pads of his thumb brushing across her trembling lips. "As if I'd want anything else in this world." His rich voice lowered to a gravelly timbre vibrating with sincerity. "I'm already halfway moved in my mind."

Prissy's breath escaped in a shuddering rush of purest relief. Looping her arms around his neck, she stretched up on her tiptoes to capture his lips in a fervent, breathtaking kiss. When they finally parted, foreheads resting together, she managed a watery chuckle. "Well then, I suppose we'd better get packing, mister."

Twinkling with unabashed glee, Alex clinked his glass to hers once more. "Absolutely. Though fair warning, darling—I do travel with rather a lot of luggage..."

THE END

acknowledgments

"**Caruso**"
written by Lucio Dalla

"**Le cygne**" (The Swan)
written by Camille Saint-Saëns

"**Shostakovich's Cello Concerto No. 1**"
written by
Dmitri Dmitriyevich Shostakovich

Sotheby's auction

Married...with Children

subscribe to our newsletter

Dive Deeper into the Stories You Love: Subscribe to the Ardent Artist Books Newsletter!

Fuel your love of fiction with exclusive content and captivating insights from Ardent Artist Books. Whether you crave the thrill of modern narratives or the timeless elegance of historical fiction, our newsletter delivers a curated selection straight to your inbox.

Here's what awaits you:

- **Exclusive Excerpts and Early Access:** Be the first to delve into upcoming releases with sneak peeks and exclusive excerpts.
- **Self-Publishing News:** Insightful KDP and IngramSpark information.
- **Genre Insights and Discussions:** Explore the nuances of modern and historical fiction with articles and discussions.

SUBSCRIBE TO OUR NEWSLETTER

Plus, as a welcome gift, receive a FREE downloadable eBook: "The Family Fix"

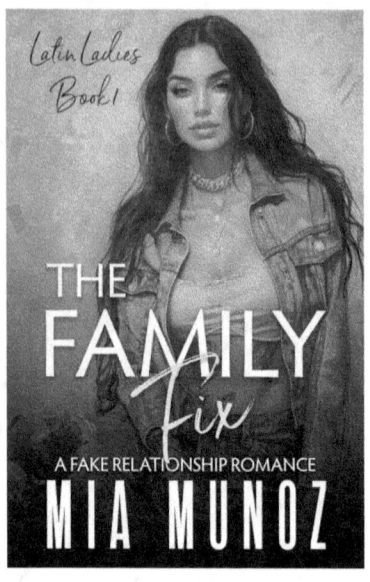

Unleash your literary passion and join our vibrant community of book lovers!
https://mailchi.mp/567874a61a56/aab-landing-page

hidden depths
A BWWM ROMANCE

HIDDEN DEPTHS: UNVEILING LOVE AND HISTORY IN THE URBAN JUNGLE

Carmina Brown, a brilliant archaeologist, unearths more than just buried artifacts in her latest dig. Her discovery of a forgotten past collides with the ambitions of **Denver Ashlen**, a ruthless real estate developer with his sights set on the very land she's determined to preserve.

An unlikely partnership forms. Carmina needs Denver's influence to protect the site, while he seeks to polish his image with philanthropic ventures. But beneath the city's bustling surface, a deeper story unfolds. Unearthed artifacts whisper tales of interracial love lost to time, sparking a connection between Carmina and Denver that mirrors the very history they uncover.

Amidst the clash of construction deadlines and the thrill of excavation, a forbidden romance blossoms. Can their love bridge the chasm between their vastly different worlds? As the weight of societal expectations and whispers of disapproval loom, Carmina and Denver must decide if their newfound passion can withstand the scrutiny of the present.

Uncover a captivating tale of love, history, and defying expectations in Hidden Depths.

COMING SOON!

A BWWM Romance

By Savannah Kole

Ebook & Paperback

the family fix
HOT NEW AUTHOR!

TIRED OF BEING THE SINGLE ONE AT FAMILY GATHERINGS?

Isabella Santos is a rising star architect with no time for love. But when her family's relentless matchmaking reaches a fever pitch, she needs a plan. Enter **Rafael Torres**, her cousin's charming best friend. A fake relationship is the perfect solution.

The problem is that pretending to be in love is a lot easier said than done.

As sparks fly and their charade heats up, Isabella and Rafael find themselves blurring the lines between pretend and reality. Can they navigate meddling families, hidden desires, and the thrill of a love that wasn't supposed to happen?

A Fake Relationship Romance

by Mia Munoz

Ebook & Paperback

a test for true love
PART TWO

Capri Harris has accepted Xavier Romano's impromptu proposal - now what? How does Xavier really feel about her?

The months ahead are now a test. Xavier introduces Capri to his parents and announces that they are getting married. Will his traditional family accept her?

Capri introduces Xavier to her parents - will her family accept him? They want to know what happened to Truett Young; they were disappointed when they heard she broke up with him; they wanted to bask in the glory and brag that their daughter was dating an NFL player.

Capri and Xavier try to navigate their feelings - did they make an impulsive decision? Capri is caught off guard when Truett returns to her life and asks for forgiveness. He proposes as well, but will Capri accept?

Xavier bumps into an old girlfriend, Maria Acosta, and old feelings begin to stir. But will Maria turn Xavier's head entirely away from Capri?

Find out what happens in **Part Two** and the continuation of **"Jealousy Never Looked So Good"**!

A BWWM Romance
by Savannah Kole
Ebook & Paperback

also by savannah

Jealousy Never Looked So Good

Sing Me a Song

Taunt Me

Crowded

Forbidden Love

Mystique

Kisser

Meet Me on Social Media

Pop Fly Kiss

The Butterfly

A Test for True Love

A Melody of Contrasts

Hidden Depths

about savannah

Savannah Kole is an author of Contemporary Romance and Modern Fiction. Savannah has many writing interests and lives an incognito digital lifestyle.

Savannah is part of the Ardent Artist Books family and is the author of several published books.

amazon.com/Ardent-Artist-Books/e/B08BX8F1DZ
youtube.com/theardentartist

www.ingramcontent.com/pod-product-compliance
Lightning Source LLC
LaVergne TN
LVHW010215070526
838199LV00062B/4602